SILVER

By Cheree L. Alsop

SILVER

To my husband, Michael Alsop.
Thank you for believing in me.

To my family for their endless support.

I love you!

SILVER

Chapter 1

I knew the contents of the trunk by heart; a brown leather jacket so worn the cloth showed through in places, an empty bottle of cologne that still held its scent, an old pair of sparing gloves with faded knuckles, and a couple of sheets of paper covered in the precise penmanship of the son of a teacher. A Hunter would kill me if he ever found the trunk, but Mom knew better than to suggest I get rid of it.

I pushed it back under my bed. My heart ached at the scent that lingered, but I forced myself to get on with unpacking. I wondered with a glance at the multitude of cardboard boxes if it was futile to pursue emptying them, but the thought of inactivity and the barrage of memories it brought sent a shudder down my spine and I turned back to work.

Night chased the shadows of evening from the street below. I couldn't see the moon through my window, but knew it would be full in a week and a half. I didn't need to look at the calendar anymore; I could feel it in my bones. I tossed several shirts into the closet and went down for dinner even though my stomach twisted at the thought of the spaghetti and meatballs that touched the air with their wheat and tomato scent.

"Do you have everything ready for school tomorrow?" Mom smiled, but her tight eyes and creased forehead belied her cheerful demeanor.

I nodded and swallowed another bite of spaghetti without tasting it.

"Did you find your backpack? I was worried you wouldn't find it in all those boxes."

The strange tone in her voice caught my attention. I looked up to see tears tracing lines down her cheeks. My heart clenched away from her pain, shoving me back into the black void I had buried myself in to survive the past couple of weeks. I couldn't let her face her pain alone, but I didn't have to face my own.

I rose and hugged her tight where she sat in her chair. She froze for a split second, then turned against my chest and started to sob. I patted her head, smoothing the long strands of dark blond hair. It was hard not to say anything, hard not to let the fire in my throat and the ache in my chest turn into its own sob, but I forced it back. A single tear traced down my cheek; I wiped it off before she saw.

"We're gonna be okay, Mom," I whispered. I stared out the kitchen window. I searched the darkness for golden eyes, but only my own image reflected back at me. It wasn't the image I held in my head.

I looked older, worn. The past two weeks had aged me more than I could have guessed. My stare reflected back hard and angry, my jaw clenched tight. Strands of blond hair fell in front of my eyes, eyes the same dark brown that dad's had been. I shook my head to clear them and turned away from my reflection, angry at the things it didn't show.

"A new school, a new territory," Mom said, her shoulders bowed. She shook her head. "You shouldn't have to go through this alone. It could be dangerous."

I couldn't help the wry tone that came to my voice. "There is no one else, Mom. I'll be okay. Who's going to mess with me?" But we both knew the truth. I stepped away. "I'll be in the backyard for a bit."

She wiped the tears from her cheeks and looked at my plate. "You're not going to finish your dinner?"

I shook my head. "Not hungry."

I didn't wait for her answer. I grabbed the pair of gloves on the counter and slid open the back door. Fresh air, so different in taste and smell it felt like we had stepped onto a different planet instead of across the country, swirled around me in an eddy of humidity, the dull roar of city night life, and a hint of rain. A cacophony of crickets, the slight breeze catching in the trees, and a pair of dogs barking at each other a few blocks away completed the portrait of night.

I strapped on the gloves and made my way to the bag I had put up the second the moving truck left. It hung from the pecan tree like a lone sentry guarding the yard against night demons. The thick paneled fence gave a facade of privacy, but it felt like eyes watched from the gaps between the wood. I shrugged off the feeling and jabbed the bag. It shook and the familiar rattle of the chain drew me back to better times. I dodged and swung. The bag rocked with the force of the blow. I stepped back and kicked it to get it moving, then ducked and punched when it came back my way.

Sweat trickled between my shoulder blades and my heart pounded by the time I finished. I leaned against the tree, my legs rubbery.

"Wear yourself out yet?"

I jumped and spun, searching the yard for any sign of movement. Lit only by stars and the faint light of the waxing moon that filtered through the reaching trees, the yard would have been nearly pitch black to anyone else; but to my eyes, shades of gray defined the shapes around me. I stood up when I confirmed that I was alone in the yard.

A faint motion between the fence panels revealed the silhouette of a person a few inches shorter than me. I stepped sideways into the slight breeze; the scent it carried, a floral perfume faint from the day, a whispered hush of mint and apricot, and a hint of pizza which I guessed was from dinner,

SILVER

confirmed that my watcher was a girl. There was nothing hostile in the scent.

I shook my head at my own fears.

"Should I take you to be the strong, silent type then?" she asked with a touch of humor.

I wasn't in the mood to be teased. "Just the type who prefers to be left alone in his own backyard." I unstrapped the gloves, the sound of the velcro loud in the silence between us. A siren wailed in the distance, followed closely by another.

"Wow, and blunt. No beating around the bush for you, huh?"

I rolled my eyes, forgetting that she couldn't see me. "Is it too much to ask for some privacy?"

"In this city? Yes, or haven't you noticed that there's barely enough room to breathe back here, let alone keep to one's self." She leaned against the fence with a huff. "What do they expect us to do after curfew, sleep?"

I laughed despite my foul mood. "I think that's the idea." I toyed with the gloves in my hands and debated whether to go in the house. The night was cool, but not the freezing temperatures I was accustomed to in early March.

"So you get all moved in?" she pressed.

I gave an inward sigh. "Yeah, pretty much."

"The moving truck wasn't there long." When I didn't answer, she waited in silence. I hoped if I kept quiet long enough she would grow bored and leave. But a few minutes later, she asked, "You starting school tomorrow?"

I frowned and fought back an urge to hit the bag again. "Yeah, why?"

"It sucks to start a new school in the middle of the year. Why'd you move?"

I turned back to the house. "Have a good night."

"You're leaving? Just like that?" She sounded surprised and a little hurt.

"Yeah, like I said, have a good night."

I took two steps when a long, low howl cut through the symphony that made up the city twilight. Dogs stopped barking, the shouts of an angry wife a few houses down quieted, and insects that had seconds ago been weaving their songs of worship to the moon fell silent. Hair rose on the back of my neck. The source wasn't close, but it was definitely werewolf. I fought the urge to bare my teeth.

The howl drifted away to a thick silence; I wondered that no other werewolf answered, then remembered that it wasn't a full moon. Uneasiness tangled under my skin at the thought of a werewolf running alone when the moon was only waxing.

"Goodnight." Her voice startled me. She made her way toward the house without waiting for a response.

"Do you have a lot of wolves here?" I wanted to kick myself as soon as the question left my mouth, but it caught her attention.

She turned and the faint light that spilled through the back door gave life to her silhouette. She had long black hair and wore loose-fitting pajama pants and a tee-shirt with a black bird printed on it. She showed her annoyance with a hand on her hip and the hard stare she gave as she tried to make out my form in the shadows.

"Oh, so now you want to talk?" she accused.

I shook my head. "Never mind."

I had reached my own back door and slid it open when she said, "Yeah, there're wolves."

I paused, a knot in my stomach. "I didn't think there would be wolves here, especially in the city." I forced my tone to lighten. "I figured there'd be more coyotes; you know, like in the westerns."

She gave an unfeminine snort. "Sorry to disappoint you. Welcome to the big city, partner." She tipped an imaginary hat my way and a laugh escaped her lips.

"Why thank you, little lady," I replied. I felt foolish, but grinned just the same.

We stared across the darkness at each other for a moment, then I stepped inside the house. "Have a good night," I called over my shoulder.

"You, too," she said.

I slid the door shut behind me and listened for her to do the same, then went upstairs for a quick shower before bed. The howl echoed through my thoughts and quickened the foreboding that rose in my chest when I thought of what the morning would bring. It was a long time before I gave in to sleep and the ever-present nightmares it heralded.

Chapter 2

I walked to school the next morning. We didn't have an extra car and Mom was out searching for a job all day; I figured the fresh air would help clear my head. The school looked normal enough from the outside. Students streamed in from buses, cars, on bikes, and on foot. The atmosphere was solemn at the early hour, and several of the seniors carried cups of coffee from the nearby Starbucks. But the similarities to my previous high school stopped when I entered the building.

Metal detectors had also decorated the entrance of my old school, but it was the cups that caught my attention. Bracelets, necklaces, rings, chains, earrings, and wrist bands, all made of silver, filled the small containers used to hold any metal that had the potential to set off the alarms. Each student that passed through the detector filled a cup nearly to the brim; two guards didn't bat an eye when one student required two cups to hold all of his silver.

The students around me threw suspicious glances my way when I passed through the detectors without putting anything in a cup. Distracted, it took two more steps for the smell to hit me.

There had been two other werewolves at my last school and we were in the same pack with eight others from around the city. It was a large pack as far as convention went. Here, my senses strained at the obvious presence of at least a dozen werewolves, enough to complete a whole pack within the school alone. My mind reeled at the implications.

The metal detectors took on a new light. Students looped necklaces and reattached bracelets with practiced ease while juggling school books and backpacks. Silver flashed in the neon glare and the light chime of metal on metal resonated harsh to my ears. The guards also wore silver, though it was much less extravagant than that of the students.

I didn't know what to make of it. I turned away, distracted, and a shoulder caught mine and shoved me into the lockers along the wall.

"Watch where you're going," a voice growled.

I looked up to see a student my age with jet black hair and dark eyes flanked by two stocky, younger students. The scent of werewolf wafted from all three of them. The student who shoved me took a step closer, then stopped; his nostrils flared and his eyes narrowed.

"You better have a good reason to be here."

I bristled at his tone. "My reasons are none of your business."

His jaw clenched and he swung at me.

The years of practice with my father paid off; my body flowed through the motions without thought. I ducked under his fist and punched as I came up, catching him in the stomach. He doubled over with a gasp, and I slammed an elbow into his back. He fell to the floor with a grunt of pain.

Arms wrapped around me from behind and squeezed tight to pin my arms to my sides. The other student punched me in the stomach with a left, then a right. I broke the student's hold and ducked, pulling his right arm over my head and behind his back. I wrapped my left arm around his throat and pulled up on his wrist. He yelped and squirmed. I pulled harder.

"Stop moving if you don't want a dislocated shoulder," I said quietly in his ear. He froze and his breath rattled in his constricted throat.

The black-haired boy struggled to his feet, his arms around his stomach. The other student hurried to his side with a hand out to help, but the boy hit it away.

"Chet Clemmons, causing trouble again are we?" The voice behind us carried a hint of frustration.

I let go of the student I held and turned, careful to keep my back to the lockers so no one could get behind me. I ignored the pain in my stomach. I had given worse than I got, evident by my first assailant's pale face and pained expression when he straightened up to talk to the man who addressed him.

"I'm not the one causing trouble, he is." He pointed at me.

Everyone's attention shifted. I hadn't realized until then how many students had stopped to watch the fight. Most had mixed expressions of excitement and foreboding, but there were a few who watched me with cold, intent stares. I forced myself to look away.

The man who spoke was of middle height, medium build, had thinning brown hair, glasses, and wore a faded brown suit that looked as though it had been washed too many times. His eyes took in the students around us with the look of someone who knew each of them by name and regarded them as his direct responsibility. He straightened his dark brown checkered tie and met my eyes with a frank, curious gaze. "I need to see you all in my office." When one of the boys started to protest, he turned and glared at the three of them. "Now."

"Yes, sir," they mumbled together.

"And if I'm not mistaken, it's time for class," he said to the onlookers. The bell rang on cue. Students broke off in groups and made their way down the hall to their various destinations. I felt several pairs of eyes on my back as I followed the three students to the office.

The man nodded at the two women behind the main desk and led us past several doors to one that stood open at the end of the hall. Glass windows made up two sides of the office and gave an excellent view of the student lounge that fronted the library. The last bell rang and two students hurried past throwing worried glances our way. The man just shook his head and sank onto a leather upholstered chair behind the l-shaped desk which bore the nameplate, 'Principal Anthony Stewart'.

The three boys took the chairs in front of the desk with the familiarity of students who had been there many times. The Principal looked up at me. "I guess we're a chair short. Do you mind grabbing one in the hall?"

"I'm okay with standing," I told him. To be honest, I felt better near the door than sitting beside three hostile werewolves. Their glares were enough to start the brawl all over again.

Principal Stewart studied me for a second, then turned back to the others. "You boys are already on thin ice. I warned you last time that one more outburst would result in suspension."

They started to protest, but he held up a hand and cut them short.

He rubbed his eyes behind his glasses with a weary sigh. "I'm feeling generous today, so take this as your last warning." He dropped his hand and looked at each of them in turn, his expression serious. "One more mistake and you're out of here. I'd better not hear of any more trouble from the three of you for the rest of the year. Understand?"

"Yes, sir," they said in sullen unison.

"Now get to class; the last thing I need is for your teachers to report you tardy."

He motioned and they left. Each one shoved past me with more force than was necessary. I smiled at their glares with a small rise of fierce satisfaction in my chest. The scent

14

of werewolf lingered in the air.

"I don't think we've met," the Principal said. I turned and found him watching me with a calculating expression. "Jaze Carso," I replied, holding out my hand. He shook with a firm grip. "Principal Stewart, if you haven't already surmised." He tipped his head toward the name plaque. "Please sit."

I took the middle seat. The odor from the cushion told of several other wolves who had sat here among countless students over the past few months.

Mr. Stewart had a file in front of him. He nodded at it. "You're the new student. I must say I didn't expect you to arrive in such a . . . tumultuous manner. You don't have any marks on your record for fighting." He met my eyes expectantly.

I shrugged and forced a nonchalant tone. "I'm normally a go with the flow kind of student. I guess I sort of . . . ."

"Didn't like where this flow was going?" he filled in.

I smiled at his easy manner. "Yeah."

He sat up in the chair and put his elbows on the desk. "May I be frank with you, Mr. Carso?"

"I would appreciate it."

"I would steer clear of Mr. Clemmons and the other students that hang around with him." He gave me a hard look as if to make sure I took him seriously.

I nodded again and wondered how much he knew. He wasn't a werewolf, that much was obvious, but he didn't act like he had the wool pulled over his eyes, either. He definitely knew something was going on in his school. I couldn't decide if that was good or bad.

He gave me a schedule and directed me toward my class, remarking offhand that with my GPA I shouldn't have too much trouble catching up. I doubted it, considering that half the school year had already passed, but decided not to press the issue.

The hallway echoed with my footsteps, and the eyes of the students in the classrooms I passed burned into my back. Banners that read, "Go Wranglers!" and, "Stomp Those Tigers!" lined the brick walls in red and gold lettering. Pictures of the basketball team were encased in glass next to a shelf of trophies, and my heart ached at the reminder of my old school.

It had been comfortable, like slipping on an old pair of shoes. I knew where everyone stood, and nobody messed with me, not because I was intimidating, but because I made it a point not to be too good at anything despite the extra strength and endurance my werewolf attributes gave me. I had a solid group of friends and the support of the pack. Everything had been perfect, until that night.

I gritted my teeth and pulled opened the door that matched the number on my schedule. Twenty-five pairs of eyes, the teacher's included, turned to me. I showed the teacher my schedule and took the seat he indicated, front and center of course, the only empty chair in the classroom. I stifled a sigh and pulled a blank notebook from my backpack.

Chapter 3

I had repeated the same scenario in three other classrooms by the time the lunch bell rang. In one, a wide berth of chairs fronting where the teacher stood was empty despite the fact that several students lounged against the back wall while they took notes. Upon taking my seat, I realized that it was the designated splash zone for a teacher who spoke with a lisp and a lot of enthusiasm. I tried in vain to shield my notebook from the splattering and vowed to get there early enough the next day so that I could get a better seat; otherwise, I would be forced to buy a parka.

I stood in line in the lunchroom and pretended to review the day's food list while I studied the layout of the room from the corner of my eye. Rows of off-white tables made up the middle of the room while shorter tables stood on either side. Students shouted insults and comments to each other across the room, much to the chagrin of the two scowling teachers that I assumed had discipline duty for the day. The scent of over-cooked French fries and salted hamburgers carried over the fainter smell of sack lunch sandwiches and potato chips.

I picked up my lunch, paid a few dollars to the bored lady with a hairnet next to an ancient computer, and carried my tray to a table near the door and a wall, a convenient location where my back would be protected. The glares of several students I passed confirmed the necessity of the position.

When I sat down, a skinny student with spiky brown hair looked up at me from his hamburger of mystery meat and squishy peas. I gave him a half-smile that I hoped came across as friendly. The last thing I needed was to be hustled during lunch.

"Welcome to our school," he said amiably. At my questioning look, he shrugged. "I work in the attendance office and saw the picture on your file. I'm Brock."

"Jaze," I said. At his nod, I shrugged, "But I guess you already knew that."

"Yeah, I'm not really supposed to see that stuff, but I can't help it if someone leaves the files lying around." He gave an affable grin, "You'd be surprised what you can find out in there. Did you know that Mr. Corley once gave a student detention for not combing his hair?" At my lack of comment, he continued, "Well, you'd have to know who Mr. Corley is to find that funny. He's bald."

His good-humor was contagious and I found myself warming up to him. It turned out that he was in my same grade, a junior. He told me he had failed his driving test for failure to yield to a cow, and had to work in the evenings to help pay for repairs on the Driver's Education car.

"Who thinks to look for a cow in the road in the Metroplex? I was being a responsible driver looking out for pedestrians and all, not searching the roads for livestock." He let out a laugh. "But the driving instructor sure saw it. He yelled so loud I think the cow might have died of fright before I even hit it!" He sighed and rolled his eyes. "But hey, it's not my fault his brake didn't work. I shouldn't have to pay for faulty school equipment, even if I was going a little fast!"

While he was talking, a voice from across the cafeteria caught my attention. Scanning the mass of unfamiliar faces, I found my neighbor at the long table against the far wall. My stomach soured when I saw who she leaned against. Chet glared at me, his dark eyes narrow. I met his gaze for a moment before reason kicked in and I turned away. This wouldn't be a good place to start another fight. I toyed briefly with Principal Stewart's comment of possible suspension, but knew better than to press my luck.

I finished my food in near silence, responding to Brock's questions with one-word answers until he turned back to the other students at the table and left me in peace. At the end of lunch, however, I was forced to ask him where to find my fifth period history class.

"You're in luck; that's my classroom, too! I can help you get caught up!" he replied with the same enthusiasm you would expect to hear from a kid who had just been told he was going to Disneyland.

I suppressed a groan and shouldered my backpack. Wary and on edge, I studied the hallways we passed. Chet and the other werewolves had finished lunch and left early; I wasn't convinced they would pass up an opportunity to seek revenge before school ended.

Fortunately, my last three classes crawled by without incident. Brock saved me a seat in Economics and took time to show me where the gym was for Physical Education even though he had Advanced English that hour. He then met me with an enthusiastic grin outside the gym doors after school.

"What'd you think of Coach Meyers?" he asked. He had a bright orange backpack slung over one shoulder, and when he turned I saw a 'kick me' sign stuck to it with gum. I pulled it off and handed it to him.

He accepted it with a casualness that said this wasn't the first time it had happened. At my questioning look, he shrugged and tossed the sign in the garbage can by the school doors. "Hey, at least they notice me," he said with a wry grin.

Two students shoved out the door past us. Anger flared in my chest and I turned, but stopped when I recognized Chet's cronies. They continued walking, but one looked back at me and gave a twisted smile. I forced myself to continue down the hall despite the rage that made me want to phase and teach them a lesson.

"Man, they sure don't like you," Brock said.

"The feeling's mutual."

"You don't want to mess with Chet's group. They're trouble." Brock sounded worried.

I fought back a grimace. "So I've been told." We stopped at my locker and I twisted the combination several times. After more than a few failed attempts, I fished the tiny slip of paper with the combination out of my pocket and tried it again. It opened with a squeak to reveal pictures of someone's girlfriend.

Brock laughed. "Guess they moved on." He took one off the door and gave it a critical look. "She's not bad." He put it in his jacket pocket. At my look, he grinned. "You never know when you might need an imaginary girlfriend to fend off some ugly chick."

"Is that something you do often?"

"It never hurts to be prepared."

I shook my head, threw my books in, and shut the door.

It was Brock's turn to stare. "Not one for studying?"

I shrugged. "Later."

"What are you doing after school?"

"We've still got a lot of unpacking to do. My mom'll be home late, so I'm going to try to get as much done as I can."

"Sounds fun," Brock said in an unconvinced tone.

I gave a wry smile. "Oh, it is; believe me."

"Well, beats working at Mack's to pay for a car I don't even get to drive."

I laughed. "Yeah, that sucks."

We walked out the front doors into the cool afternoon air. The parking lot quickly emptied as students and teachers rushed to leave school. We made our way along the row of buses to the side road.

I turned toward home, "See ya later."

"Hey," Brock said over his shoulder. "If you get bored, come by the shop."

I paused on the sidewalk. "You walking there?"

He grinned. "No license, remember? Besides, it's not that far."

I thought about it. If Mom's job search didn't go well, she might be out late anyway and I definitely didn't have anything else to do. I nodded. "I might stop by."

"It's just up Main past First Street."

"Got it."

He shoved his hands in his pockets and continued down the road.

I made my way toward home, but a few streets later realized that was the last place I wanted to go. Nothing was more depressing than a house full of boxes. Mom wouldn't mind if I unpacked later.

I jogged west through some apartment buildings and up a road between rundown brick warehouses so I could meet up with Brock before he reached the shop. Someone yelled and I stopped short. I strained my ears to hear the voice again.

"What do you want with me?" Brock's words were strained.

I ran through an alley on my left in time to see Brock back up against a wall with his hands raised. Two boys and a big animal stood with their backs to me. I recognized two of Chet's followers and realized with a jolt of surprise that the animal with them was a werewolf already phased to wolf form.

"Chet wants to know about that Jaze kid. You've been hanging around him all day like a lovesick puppy."

"No!" Brock shook his head. "I don't know anything, I swear."

21

The first boy grinned. "I don't believe you. And Chet said to get answers any way we could." He took a step forward. The wolf beside him lowered its head. A fierce growl ripped from its throat.

"Whoa." Brock leaned back against the wall, his eyes wide. "I don't know what you want, and I don't know anything about Jaze except that he just moved here. That's all, I swear it!"

"Oh, you'll be doing more than swearing by the time we're done with you," the second boy said with a cruel laugh. He pulled his shirt off.

A voice inside my head screamed for me to walk away, but I ignored it and entered the alley. "Leave him alone."

The boys and wolf looked back at me in surprise. I made my way toward them with calm, measured steps despite the adrenaline that pounded through my veins. I met Brock's eyes; fear and relief reflected in them. He shook his head as if to tell me to leave and save myself. I gave him a grim smile. "Looks like the boys at your school don't know how to play nice."

"Jaze, get outta here," Brock said. The wolf turned and snapped at him. He leaned back into the brick wall.

"You know," I said, my tone fierce with anger I could barely control, "If you have questions, you could have asked me."

The two boys exchanged crooked smiles at my invitation. The one with his shirt off started toward me. "That can be arranged." He phased in a blur of skin and fur. His teeth sharpened and mouth elongated into a pointed muzzle. His shoulders rolled and ears moved to higher points on his head. His legs and arms bent and shifted their muscles, forcing him onto all fours. His pants fell discarded at his feet. A growl rolled from his throat. I looked into the golden eyes of the gray wolf and saw the animal hunger in them. He gathered his legs under his body to leap.

I pulled off my shirt phased into wolf form in the split second it took for him to leave the ground. His eyes widened, but it was too late for him to change course. He slammed into my shoulder. I rolled with the force of the collision while his own momentum threw him over me and into the trashcans along the wall.

The other boy had phased to wolf form by the time I got to my feet. I backed slowly so that I had a wall behind me and could watch all three wolves. Their coats were varying shades of gray, male wolves who didn't wear the black of an Alpha. The one that had tangled with the garbage cans limped back over to join his pack mates. I sensed their confusion, a mixture of anger and surprise at my black Alpha fur. There was no time for them to regroup with Chet and decide what their next course of action should be.

Three heads lowered, ears flat and hackles lifted. I bared my teeth. A low growl rumbled from my chest. I could see Brock pressed against the wall out of the corner of my eye. The fear that rolled off him in waves fueled my rage. Fire flowed through my veins as the three wolves leaped.

I ducked under the first wolf and caught the shoulder of the next in my jaws. I shook him and threw his body against the nearest wall. He yelped and fell to a heap on the ground. The third wolf grabbed my forearm in his mouth and bit down. His sharp teeth tore through the flesh; pain laced up to my shoulder. A snarl ripped from my throat and I turned and bit at his neck. My teeth sought purchase through the thick fur. The scent of his panic filled my nose. He let go and darted back, breaking my hold.

The first wolf dove at me again. I jumped to the side and his teeth missed by inches. Before he could regain his footing,

I used my shoulder to bowl him over. His belly was exposed and he yelped in fear. I latched onto his unprotected throat. My ears filled with sound of his blood pounding millimeters from my teeth. I growled a warning.

He froze. A strained whine escaped him. I heard his two pack mates' anxious replies. My jaws ached to close, to end his life in an effort to release some of the fury and anger pent up inside me, but I fought against it. I growled again for good measure, and then let up the pressure. The wolf on the ground held still for another moment. When he realized I wasn't going to attack, he rolled onto his belly and slunk back to his pack mates. They left the alley without a sound. I noted with grim satisfaction that two of them limped, and the third held his tail between his legs.

Movement from the corner of my eye snuffed out the satisfaction. Brock detached himself from the wall; his eyes never left me when he leaned down to pick up his backpack. The fear in his gaze left me hollow.

I turned and made my way back through the alley. Blood ran down my front leg where the wolf's teeth had scored it and I tried not to limp. Normally, I would phase back to human form in an effort to be less conspicuous in the city, but I had left my clothes in the alley and couldn't bring myself to go back for them. I wondered if a naked human or a huge wolf would catch more attention. I settled on the rationale that most people could accept a wolf as a large sled dog. A naked human was not so easily overlooked.

Regardless of all that had happened, it felt good to be back in wolf form. I hadn't phased since the last time with my dad. Though the full moon next week would make it inevitable, Dad and I had always escaped a few nights a week for a run. Being back in wolf form after the past two weeks felt like stretching muscles that had been too long dormant. I relished the feeling, and phased to human form only when I realized our back door wasn't easy to open with a muzzle and paws.

I pulled on some pants and sat in the kitchen attempting to bandage my still bleeding arm when the doorbell rang. I tied off the cloth and slipped on a shirt with long sleeves before I made my way to the door. My heart slowed when I opened it to find Brock, my discarded clothes tucked under one arm.

Trepidation rose in my chest. "What are you doing here?" I growled.

"You saved my life, man. The least I could do is return your clothes." Brock pushed past me into the house.

I stared after him in surprise, then shook my head, shut the door, and followed him to the living room. Boxes filled most of the sitting areas, and he turned back to me with raised eyebrows. "You really did just move here, didn't you?"

"Saturday. Why?"

He shrugged. "I was wondering on the way over if it was some story to cover up an underground werewolf something-or-other." His eyes lit up. "Did you move here because of a werewolf thing?"

My eyes narrowed. "It's none of your business."

He held up his hands, a grin on his face. "Okay, okay. If you don't want to talk about it, that's fine." He pushed aside a stack of books and sat on the corner of the couch. At my look, he apologized. "Sorry. I keep feeling like I'm going to fall over. A long walk after being attacked by werewolves must not have been good for me."

I studied him. "It's not that long of a walk."

"If you have four feet, maybe. But I had to make it on two," he said casually as if he often made references to werewolves.

"Have you ever seen a werewolf before?"

25

He shook his head. "Never, and not for lack of trying."

That surprised me. "You mean, you've *tried* to find werewolves?"

"Oh, yeah." He sat up, his expression brightening. "Mouse and I have been trying to find proof of werewolves for as long as I can remember. It's a hobby of ours."

"Strange hobby," I muttered. I frowned. "But you can't tell him. No one can know."

"Word'll spread fast enough to Chet if I know Max and Darryl." His tone turned pleading. "Are you sure I can't tell Mouse? He'd be thrilled to know we were right all along."

I shook my head. "Absolutely not. You're lucky to still be alive. No human is supposed to know of the presence of a werewolf. Chet's followers would have killed you when they'd gotten all they could out of you."

Brock's eyes widened, then narrowed. "But you could have let them kill me and didn't. Don't you follow werewolf law?"

I gritted my teeth. "I'm not so fond of it at the moment."

"Is that the reason you moved out here?"

I shook my head and made my way to the kitchen to clean up before Mom got home. Blood on the counters was the last thing she needed to see after a hard day of job hunting. "I told you I'm not talking about it."

"Okay." He followed me, then stopped at the sight of the blood. "Whoa. I didn't think you got hurt."

I raised my sleeve to show him the already soaked bandage before I turned away to find a rag in the cupboards.

"I thought werewolves healed quickly."

His knowledge concerned me, but I didn't let it show. "We do, but it still takes some time." I found a rag, ran it under the tap, then began blotting at the counter top.

He fell silent. I looked up to see him watching me.

"Thank you," he said quietly, his expression sincere.

"Don't mention it." I finished the counters and rinsed the rag in the sink. Blood ran over my hands when I wrung it out. The water turned pink as it carried away the iron scent. I tossed the rag into the washing machine by the bathroom.

Brock followed me down the hall. "So what now?"

"What do you mean, what now?"

"Well, do you wage war on them or something?"

I shook my head and walked back to the kitchen. "There's too many of them. I shouldn't even be here. The most I can hope is for them to ignore me from here on out."

Brock looked disappointed. "Oh." Then he perked up again. "But what if they don't?"

I turned to face him, exasperated. "Why do you want me to fight them so bad?"

"Because I finally have proof that there are werewolves, and now everything's just going to go back to normal? I don't think so." His voice softened, his face pale. "According to you, Chet's gang will have to kill me now that I know what they are."

The thought turned my stomach. He was right. I took a seat at the table. Brock hesitated, then did the same.

His eyebrows lifted. "Hey, if they had bitten me, would I turn into a werewolf, too?"

I shook my head. "No. That's just a myth. Werewolves are born, not made."

"Then why the rumors?"

I shrugged and ran my finger along a small rip in the yellow flower print tablecloth that still smelled of our old home. "It's their attempt to be thought of as human instead of monsters."

Brock gave me a strange look and I realized I had said 'their' instead of 'our'.

I rose from the table and my chair slid back with a screech. Brock jumped, but his face was carefully expressionless, his eyes on mine. "You wanna watch a movie?"

I took a deep breath and let it out with an exasperated huff. "You aren't afraid of me?"

He shook his head. "Should I be?"

I glanced out the window in search of an answer. My reflection stared back. I sighed and turned again to Brock. "No, not of me. But you're right about Chet's pack. I suggest you start carrying some real silver."

Brock's eyes widened. "You mean it really works?"

I gave him a tight-lipped smile. "Unless you strike a vital organ, silver won't kill. But we're allergic to it. Especially the weaker members of a pack." At his questioning look, I explained. "Alphas have black fur, and the rest of the male werewolves' fur ranges from dark gray to light gray. The lighter it is, the weaker they are."

Brock thought it over for a minute, then his eyes lit with the question I knew was coming. "So you're. . . ."

I nodded.

Brock sat back in his chair. "Wow, an Alpha. No wonder Chet's gang doesn't like you."

I shrugged. "Something I'll have to deal with on my own." I changed the subject. "Any suggestions for a movie?"

A smile spread across Brock's face. "How about 'Teenwolf'?"

"Very funny."

Chapter 4

I stifled a smile at the surprised look on Mom's face when she found Brock and I hanging out in the box-cluttered living room, but she recovered quickly and asked if he would like to join us for dinner.

"Absolutely. What are we having?" Brock shot me a questioning look.

I shook my head. No, my mom was definitely not a werewolf, and he wouldn't have to worry about rare steaks for dinner.

The obvious disappointment on Brock's face turned into excitement when Mom mentioned she was making chicken Alfredo manicotti. She met my eyes, a sad smile on her lips. An answering pang tore through my chest. It was a dish Dad and I always requested, one of my favorites. Her smiled firmed with a determination that said she was not going to let everything pleasant go. I nodded an agreement that I didn't feel.

Brock didn't notice our unspoken exchange. He followed Mom into the kitchen like a starving puppy and asked how he could help speed things along. I shook off the heavy weight I felt and tagged behind.

Brock didn't seem to mind the time it took to make the food. He helped Mom cut and clean vegetables, grate cheese, and prepare the filling. I was put to work with a bowl of cookie batter. My culinary shortcomings had been accepted long ago, but Mom said I had a special skill in spooning dollops of batter onto a pan. Demeaning, yes, but I conceded because it was better than nothing.

I watched Mom and Brock at the bar and tried not to remember my tall, confident father who should have been beside her. I looked down at the mixture I stirred and it was hard not to pretend that he was with us again, telling his jokes and stories.

Mom laughed and I stood up so fast my chair fell over with a crash.

"Jaze, what's wrong?" she asked, surprised.

Brock froze with his knife midway through a head of broccoli. He looked from Mom to me, but I couldn't meet their eyes. "I was just telling her about the cow," he said.

I slammed the bowl down, angry at myself for letting my emotions get the better of me. But before I could say anything, a sound cut through the room.

The howl was deep and angry, like a tin roof torn open during a hurricane. It was a challenge.

The hair rose on the back of my neck. My lips pulled back in a snarl. I stepped around the table.

"Jaze, no!" Mom and Brock said at the same time.

"He's out there!" I was barely aware that I was shouting. I stared past them toward the front door. "He knows where we live!" My chest heaved and I fought not to phase.

"You can't take them by yourself," Brock argued. He grabbed my arm.

I stared at him for a moment without seeing him. Blood pounded in my ears. I wanted to phase, wanted it more than anything I could remember. The anger that I had tried to keep down the last few weeks boiled through me like hot tar. I needed to rip into something, to tear it apart to match my soul.

The howl sounded again, but it was mixed with many others, a whole pack of werewolves that circled our front yard.

"Jaze?"

The fear in Mom's voice broke through the dissonance of my mind. I blinked and saw Mom and Brock in front of me, their eyes on the front door. I realized what I had almost done and steadied myself with a shaky hand against the table. "They're leaving," I whispered. The slight change in the tone of the howls, too subtle for human ears, renewed the threat, then faded; they left into a night which had become much darker.

I fell into a chair and put my face in my hands, my elbows on the table. I closed my eyes and waited for my heart to stop hammering in my ears. The howls echoed in my head and refused to fade.

The oven chime sounded and I jumped. I took a deep breath and pushed down the urge to run after the werewolves, to defend my territory and my family against all the hatred I heard in their voices. I grabbed the bowl again in an effort to calm my mind. "I'm not quite ready with the cookie dough."

"What was that?" Mom's voice shook.

"A new territory," I replied in an even tone. I met her eyes, my own carefully concealing my thoughts. "We knew this would be coming."

She shook her head, a spark of anger in her eyes now. "No, not like this. Not at our own house."

"They're not happy I'm here, and they want to deal with it like animals."

"Then we're leaving," Mom said. "There are too many of them."

"I'm not leaving." The edge in my voice surprised us both. I tried to sort out my conflicting emotions. "What's to say it won't be like this at another school in another city? We have to try to ride it out here."

"And what if they don't let you?" Mom asked with a frustrated gesture toward the front door.

"I'll work it out."

"And he won't be alone."

I had forgotten Brock was there. I stared at him with a faint spark of amusement at the thought that he would watch my back against the wolves.

Mom looked at him with a hand on her hip. "Are you a werewolf too?" She glared at me. "Are you inviting strangers into this house who could turn on us?"

A laugh burst out of me at the thought of Brock as a werewolf. Mom's answering glower only made the situation more hilarious.

After his initial surprise, Brock laughed too. "I'm definitely not a werewolf," he said when he stopped to catch his breath.

I shook my head. "Far from it." Brock threw me a grin.

I stirred the batter again, feeling somewhat better. I could still sense Mom glaring at me and gave her a placating smile. "It's okay, Mom. They're not going to kill me. They're still held to the Law."

"But there are so many of them."

"All the more reason for none of them to cross the line. They won't want their pack broken up by force."

I could tell she wasn't satisfied, but she let the argument go. She grabbed hot-pads and carried manicotti and steamed vegetables to the table.

Brock took a seat next to me and, at Mom's invitation, helped himself to the food. He raved at each bite about how good the food tasted.

Mom smiled despite the concern that furrowed her brow. "Doesn't your mom cook?"

Brock nodded and said around a mouthful of broccoli, "Yeah, she cooks the same thing every night. It's amazing how many kinds of frozen pizza there are!"

Mom laughed, then embarrassment colored her face when she realized it wasn't a joke.

"Don't worry, Mrs. C," Brock said, mistaking her expression. "Your manicotti's better than frozen pizza any day."

I burst out laughing.

***

At Mom's insistence, Brock let us drive him home. Though he put on a brave front, worry showed on his face at the thought of school tomorrow. "I get bored walking by myself. Do you mind if I swing by and get you on the way? You're only a few blocks down," I offered before he left the car.

"You mean it?" he asked, his eyes bright.

I nodded and he gratefully accepted, then ran through the dark to his front door without looking back.

"I feel the same way," Mom said quietly. She waited to make sure Brock shut and locked the door before she drove away.

"He's had quite the rude awakening," I agreed. "He's brave though."

Mom drove down the street in silence, her lips pressed together in a tight line. I turned to look out the window, but changed my mind when a shadow detached itself from the others to run alongside our car.

"I'm enrolling you in karate lessons."

"I can't take karate, Mom. I'm too strong. It would be obvious." I forced myself to look back out the window. The shadow was gone.

"Then how else are you supposed to defend yourself?"

"Dad taught me, remember?" I tried not to sound bitter. "I can take care of myself. I already won one fight today." I threw it in as a jab, but regretted it the moment it left my mouth.

Mom's eyes widened and she stared at me. "You fought today? With werewolves?" Her voice rose. "Were you hurt? Was anyone killed?"

I shook my head quickly to cut off her barrage of questions. "Three werewolves tried to get information from

34

Brock about me. They would have killed him if I hadn't stepped in. They'd already phased, Mom, and in broad daylight."

Her mouth fell open. "He saw them? He saw you?"

I nodded. "If I hadn't phased, he would've been a body in an alley. It makes me wonder how often that happens around here." Mom's jaw tightened and I could tell she was about to begin her argument about moving away again. The car inched slowly toward the other lane of traffic as she focused all her attention on me.

"And that's why I can't leave," I pressed, the thoughts that had been racing around my head finally settling into a semblance of order. "Something's wrong here, and until I find what's at the bottom of it, I can't go. There're too many innocent lives at stake." I grabbed the wheel and eased the car back onto our side of the street. Luckily, it was late and no one else seemed to be out. Mom had a tendency to go under the speed limit anyway, and I doubted we would do much harm at 15 miles per hour.

Mom opened her mouth, then closed it again and turned to face forward. I let go of the wheel and sat back. That was it, what had been bothering me. There were too many werewolves here. The general population had some notion that they existed; otherwise, why all the silver at school if not to prove that the wearer wasn't a werewolf? But werewolves could tolerate thin grades of silver; the plated metal on most jewelry wouldn't cause more than a slight rash after being worn for a day.

My bigger worry was the fact that Chet would send his pack after a student without fear of repercussion. Had this happened before? Or was this wolf pack thicker into the city's politics than I imagined?

I figured the best place to start would be the files at school. Even if the principal didn't know what was going on, there had to be some mention in the files of abnormal activity.

Chapter 5

The wolves didn't come back that night, but I was jarred from sleep time and again by howls that echoed all too real in my dreams. I didn't feel at all rested by the time I got up. I found a discarded silver wristband with spikes in one of my junk boxes and put it on. I felt Mom's eyes on it when I came down for breakfast.

"Going to meet up with Brock?"

I had to give her credit for the effort. I could tell by the lines around her eyes that she had been up worried all night. "Yeah; otherwise, I think he might skip school." I didn't mention that I toyed with the same idea. I sat down at the table and forced myself to eat a few bites of the cereal she had poured for me.

Mom walked behind where I sat and surprised me by leaning down and putting her arms around me from behind. "Take care of him, Jaze," she said quietly. "Take care of you both. I can't pretend to be okay with this, but I know you have your reasons. Just give me the option to say enough if it goes overboard."

I could hear the pain in her voice, the fear of losing another member of her family. A lump formed in my throat and I nodded. She squeezed my shoulders, then let go with a sigh.

A smile tugged at the corners of her lips when she walked around the table to face me. She rested her hands on the back of a chair. "You have so much of your father in you. He never would back down from a fight. I think it's the Alpha in you."

I grinned at her. "That's what you get for marrying the toughest werewolf in town."

She nodded. "You got that right."

It felt good to talk like we used to, even though we both forced it for the other's sake. It would be a long time before anything felt natural again.

***

I fought back a grin as I pulled off the silver wristband and dropped it in a cup before I passed through the metal detectors. Brock filled his own cup most of the way and followed me through. The students around us didn't pay any attention, though I could tell by the feral odor in the air that several of Chet's werewolves had chosen to tag along. We walked down the hall with forced nonchalance, and I refrained from pointing out our followers to Brock. He already looked pale, but I had to give him credit for meeting me in front of his house ready for whatever the day might bring.

My locker, situated down a side hall, would have been the perfect place for an ambush. I passed the hallway and continued to my classroom despite the fact that I didn't have my books. Brock threw me a sideways glance, but didn't argue.

We had almost reached Brock's first class, Algebra II, which happened to be across from my Science class, when I heard footsteps. I turned and ducked; our first attacker doubled over my shoulder and I rose to send him crashing into the lockers that lined the hall. Then they surrounded us.

My nerves tingled at the scent of silver, pure silver, not the cheap stuff that plated most of the jewelry the students wore. Knives flashed in the grip of at least three of our attackers. Chet was serious about this. I stepped in front of Brock, who knew better than to protest, and widened my stance. Feeling foolhardy and in a bad mood, I gestured for them to bring it on.

Chet's pack dove at me in a group. I caught a dozen punches and kicks, and gave only half that, but with my Alpha strength those I gave left a mark. I felt bone crunch under my knuckles and a werewolf cried out in pain. A punch caught me on a cheekbone. I dove out of the fray toward my attacker, and his triumphant expression turned to fear when he saw me coming. I threw a two-fisted punch at his chest; he slammed back against the wall and slid to the floor. Arms grabbed me from behind before I could finish him. I tripped over someone's legs and fell onto my back. An elbow slammed into my stomach and my breath left in a gasp. I fought for air, my arms above my face to protect it from the blows. Fists and shoes battered my unprotected ribs.

Then a knife cut along my side and fire exploded through my veins. Thunder pounded in my ears and I fought not to phase. The punches and kicks became nothing more than goads for my anger. Before the phase could take over, I jumped to my feet, throwing those who were closest to me into the surrounding wall of students.

I used the adrenaline that compelled me to phase and attacked Chet's pack. The ten or so werewolves must have felt the change in me. They fell back against the students who watched the fight with opened mouths, and scrambled to break through the tightly packed ranks. My vision flared red and I threw my assailants right and left. I found two silver knives in unresisting hands and threw them hilt-deep into the nearest classroom door. I grabbed two werewolves and was about to smash their heads together when the Principal's voice rang out.

"Mr. Carso!"

His tone broke through the red haze. I shook my head to clear my eyes, and looked up to find him inside the ring of students, his hands clenched into fists. Even though he had said my name, he glared at the students around me like it was their fault I had beaten them. His gaze finally rested on me. "I would like to see both of you in my office."

CHEREE ALSOP

I looked behind me and was glad to see Brock cowering unharmed by the door. He gave me a weak smile and ran a hand through his sweaty hair. I helped him to his feet, then staggered back as the fading adrenaline left my body. Brock caught my arm, his eyes wide. We shouldered through the watching students.

"Thanks, man," I said low enough so the other students couldn't hear.

"No prob," Brock replied with a shrug and a shadow of his easy smile.

Most of the students left to class. The second bell gave a shrill ring, leaving Chet's pack members to help each other to the nurse's office. I wondered why Principal Stewart didn't call them to his office as well, but decided not to press my luck by asking. I didn't think I was the only one who noticed Chet missing from the group.

Principal Stewart led the way into his office. I took the same seat I had the day before, and fought back a grimace at the irony. "A second fight in two days, and with Mr. Clemmons' group again? I'm a little surprised." But his expression was far from surprised. The Principal laced his fingers together and leaned forward on his desk. He glanced sideways at Brock, hesitated, then sighed. "Jaze, I'm sorry about your father. Your old school sent the records over this morning."

My heart slowed, and I clenched my fists behind the desk where he couldn't see them. They ached, but it felt good, an ache to get lost in. The burning fire from the shallow wound the silver knife had left along my side flared whenever I moved. My shirt stuck to my side and I was suddenly grateful I wore black because the blood wouldn't show through as easily.

Brock nudged me with his elbow and I looked up to see Principal Stewart watching me with an expectant expression. "Sorry, sir. Can you repeat the question?"

The Principal gave an understanding smile. "Where did you learn to fight like that?"

I was glad he changed the subject from my father. "I came from a hard town." I didn't say that I had just moved to a harder one.

He nodded. "Well, I'm glad that you can take care of yourself. I don't condone fighting in the school, but I especially hate to see someone outnumbered." He shook his head. "Maybe they'll try to stay on your good side from now on."

I smiled. "Doubt it."

Principal Stewart looked down at my arm. "What happened there."

"Dog bit me yesterday," I said quickly. I glanced down at the mostly-healed gouges, then looked up at the Principal again.

"Yesterday?"

It was too late to change my story, so I nodded.

His eyebrows rose, but he didn't press it. "You two had better get to class if you're up to it, or I could have the nurse excuse you for the day."

The thought of a walk home with werewolves at our heels was more than I could handle at the moment. "No thank you, sir," I said.

"We'll be fine at class," Brock agreed; his voice squeaked on the word class, but neither of us laughed.

I could feel the Principal's eyes on us as we walked back down the hall. I didn't want to know what he was thinking.

Chapter 6

Brock followed me into the restroom. I made sure it was empty, then propped a garbage can under the door handle to wedge it shut. I eased off my shirt to assess the damage from the silver knife.

Brock had gone straight to the sink to splash water on his face, and when he saw me in the mirror, he turned, his face dripping. "Dang, man!"

I grabbed some paper towels and ran them under the water. "Leave it to Chet to bring out the silver weapons."

Brock's eyes widened. "But aren't werewolves allergic to silver?"

I nodded and squeezed the excess water out of the towels before turning to inspect my side. The cut was shallow but long. It ran down my right side from the middle of my ribs to just above my hip bone. Blood oozed slowly down and I wiped it away. I clenched my teeth and held the wound open with my right hand while attempting to scrub it out with the paper towels in my left. I hit a particularly sensitive spot where a shard of silver was embedded and sucked in a quick breath at the stab of pain.

"Give me that." Brock took the towels from me, threw them away, and got a fresh set. He worked at the spot for a moment, his jaw tight. When he finally worked the offender free, he held it up for inspection. "More silver?"

I motioned for him to throw it in the garbage and set a hand against the wall to steady myself. "Knives for battle against werewolves are designed to splinter. It leads to a slow, agonizing death if the wound isn't cleaned." He found another sliver and I clenched my fist against the gray bricks. "Usually, it's the Hunters who use them, not werewolves against each other."

Brock met my gaze in the mirror. "I guess you've found an especially amiable pack, then."

I snorted. "Lucky me."

The bleeding had stopped for the most part by the time he finished. I pulled my shirt back on and turned to open the door, but Brock put a hand on the garbage can that blocked it.

"What happened to your dad?"

I shook my head and pushed the garbage can aside, but he leaned against the door. My first impulse was to throw him like I had done to several members of Chet's pack. I closed my eyes and took a deep breath, trying to find the calm void I had created around the pain. "I don't want to go there."

Brock crossed his arms and gave me a frank stare. The fact that he dared to stand up to me made me appreciate his bravery even more. "Look, Jaze. Something bad obviously happened, and you can't carry it all by yourself." He kicked a heel against the door. "Mouse's parents were killed in a car accident a few years ago, and it was all I could do to keep him from running away or doing something crazy. We all need a shoulder once in a while."

His words clicked, and I felt the tiniest bit of relief that someone even cared. I couldn't talk to Mom, because she already cried in her bed at night when she thought I was asleep. The helpless emotions welled up inside me like a shaken bottle of soda. It was a slim thing that I hadn't phased and torn into Chet's pack. I had to talk to someone to relieve some of the tension I carried.

I shoved my hands in my pockets and leaned against the cold tile wall. My side stung, but I ignored it. I studied the dirty floor. "He was killed by Hunters two weeks ago." I forced my voice to be calm despite the knot in my throat. "Mom and I had gone out to eat because Dad had to work late. We went bowling afterwards, and when we got home, the front door was open."

I shut my eyes against the flood of memories. Blood coated our walls in ragged spurts. I could see my dad's arm behind Mom's rocking chair where she used to hum while she cross-stitched. His torso had been thrown into the fireplace; ashes mixed with the dark blood. We never found his head.

Brock set a hand on my arm, jarring me back to the present. "I'm sorry, man," he said quietly.

"You know what the worst part is?" I looked at him but still saw the violent scene in the living room. The metallic scent of blood filled my nose along with another scent, one that haunted me. "I think my uncle was behind it."

Brock opened his mouth to speak, then shut it again.

I ground my teeth in an effort to keep calm. "My dad was the leader of our pack, and my uncle was his second. He supported my dad in everything, but Dad told me once that he thought it was just a show, that his brother wanted power. He told me later to forget about it, but I never did." I took a deep breath. "The night my dad was killed, I smelled him there. A werewolf would never work with a Hunter, but I know he had something to do with it."

Anger filled my chest. I wanted to phase and rip something apart so bad it hurt. I grabbed the metal paper towel holder and ripped it off the wall, then threw it against one of the stalls hard enough to put a rectangular dent in its side. I turned and did the same with the hand dryer, leaving only stray wires sticking out where the machine had been. I fought to catch my breath, and slid down against the wall until I sat on the floor.

The paper towel holder sprung open with a click that made both Brock and I jump. Paper towels flew out like confetti. One landed on my knee. I picked it up and started to laugh. Brock sat down against the door and started laughing, too.

"That's one paper towel holder we won't have to worry about," he said.

"Yeah," I managed to get out. "And the blow dryer won't be messing with anyone, either."

I held my side, which objected to the movement of my ribs as I laughed, but I couldn't stop. It was like the pent-up anger had to get out somehow and was glad to have found a non-violent, or less-violent, release. When I finally pushed up to my feet, my stomach hurt from laughing and the knife wound burned like fire, but I felt a little better.

Brock grinned at me. "See, it helps to talk and throw stuff across the room."

I glanced back at the destroyed appliances and dented stall. "We'd better get out of here before they come asking questions."

"Good idea."

We ran down the hall to our separate classrooms, and I ducked through the door to Science. Two werewolves glared at me, but I ignored them and took a seat in the far corner. The werewolves weren't the only ones who watched me; I heard whispered descriptions of the fight told to those who had missed it. Unfortunately, there was no need to embellish on the details. My own aggression after the knife incident provided plenty to talk about.

I slumped in my chair and attempted to pay attention to the teacher's rehashed description of Photosynthesis, a topic I swear had been beaten to death by middle school and did little to keep me from reliving the fight in my own mind. The details blurred but my knuckles pulsed at each remembered connection with flesh; my side burned and adrenaline pounded through my veins as I felt the knife wound again. It didn't help that the student in front of me had the fight recorded on his phone and sent it to his neighbor, who unfortunately was one of the werewolves I had pummeled. He glared at me, but the first student gave me a thumbs-up.

"This'll be all over the school by lunch," he whispered excitedly.

"Mr. Morrison," the teacher said in a threatening growl. "You better not be texting during class."

The student sat up. "No, Mrs. Poller. I was just making sure the new guy wasn't lost."

The teacher stared at him for a minute, then nodded. "Alright then." She turned back to the whiteboard.

***

It was like that until lunch. Students watched the fight and talked about it in, during, and between classes. I saw myself wipe the floor with Chet's pack from several different angles and heard accounts that made me sound like Superman. I sat my tray down on the table next to Brock for lunch and groaned.

"Bombarded about the fight?" Brock asked. When I nodded, he smiled sympathetically. "Hey, at least they realize you were there. The most I get is, 'Good thing you were on his side.' Very demeaning if you ask me."

"Very," I mumbled into my lasagna of questionable origin.

I looked across the lunchroom and found the Alpha wolf sitting in his usual corner with his pack around him. I took a grim pride in the fact that several of them were bandaged and bruised and shot glares in my direction. But when they saw I was looking, they turned away and ignored me.

I sat back and toyed with my food. Brock glanced at me once in a while, but he left me in silence. Then Mouse sat down.

Mouse was small and scrawny like his nickname. He had light brown hair and glasses, and brought a sack lunch. Everything about him was puny, except the smell. He was definitely a werewolf.

At my surprised look, Mouse gave a minute shake of his head. I stifled a laugh at the fact that Brock was so interested in werewolves, and his friend who had been part of the search for information was in fact one.

Brock turned the topic to a new thriller movie about vampires that was releasing next weekend, leaving me to my own thoughts. I studied Mouse who kept his eyes on his peanut butter and jelly sandwich. The boy looked sick but relieved that I didn't rat him out. When the bell rang, he hurried away. He avoided any contact with Chet's pack, which was also peculiar.

Chapter 7

"Maybe they've decided not to mess with you," Brock said hopefully when we reached his house after school. "Maybe," I said, but I doubted it. They would probably take a few days to lick their wounds and wounded pride, but two Alphas never lived peaceably in the same city for long. Lucky for Brock, he told his parents about the attack the other day in the alley but made it seem like an attempted mugging instead of a werewolf death threat. They forbade him from going to Mack's anymore, paid off his debt on the car, and set up chores for him to do at home instead. They also treated me like royalty, making me wonder what Brock had said about his 'rescue'.

"Some pepperoni pizza to take home?" Mrs. Nelson asked, hurrying out the door after us with a large sandwich bag.

"Uh, sure," I replied. She had sent me off that morning with a breakfast pizza of cheesy scrambled eggs and sausage when I picked up Brock. I had been grateful for it, but this was getting ridiculous. "You know you don't have to-"

She cut me off and shoved the overflowing bag into my hands. "Now, now, every growing boy likes pizza, don't they, Brock?" She ruffled his hair and gave him a fond smile.

Brock grimaced and threw me an apologetic look.

I shrugged. "Thanks, Mrs. Nelson. I really appreciate it."

"Enjoy, and don't forget to tell your Mom that we would love to have you over for dinner some night."

"I will." I hurried away before she could tie me into any other commitments.

"He's a nice kid," I heard her say to Brock. He mumbled something and they disappeared into the house. I breathed a sigh of relief when the screen door creaked shut behind them.

***

Mom had left a note on the counter. "Found a job, have to go to training tonight. There's leftovers in the fridge and some money on the counter if you want pizza. I love you. Keep safe."

I filled a cup of milk and took a couple of Mrs. Nelson's pizza slices into the living room to watch TV, but I couldn't relax. I ordered Chinese food, figuring that Mom would understand if I didn't get more pizza, then paced by the door until the delivery boy showed up. Unfortunately, he turned out to go to our school.

"Hey, it's you!" he said when I opened the door.

I stifled a groan and handed him the twenty Mom had left.

"I was there during the fight. You sure pounded those guys!" He gave a serious frown. "But I don't know if I'd go up against them. That Chet's a bad guy to mess with."

"Tell me about it," I said under my breath.

"Huh?"

I shook my head. "Nothing. Thanks for the food." I shut the door before he could protest.

"Hey, what about your change?" he shouted through the door.

"Keep it!"

It must have been more than I thought, because a second later a surprised, "Thanks, man!" sounded.

I sighed, sat back down on the couch, and began to flip through the channels in the search of something interesting. I ate half the food while watching a documentary on dingoes, then threw the bag in the fridge. The clock showed 10:33pm. It was past curfew, but I wasn't tired. I went in the backyard and punched the bag a few times to work out the soreness in my knuckles from the fight, but when I turned with a punch the knife wound opened and started to bleed again. I gave up.

The neighbor's back door opened. The scent of Chet's girl tangled through the air.

"Where are you going?" a woman's voice shouted after her.

"Nowhere," she yelled back. "There's nowhere to go." She let the screen door slam shut behind her and walked to the middle of the yard where she stopped with her arms crossed tightly in front of her chest.

"Parent problems?"

She turned and glared in my direction. "What business is it of yours?"

"None." I shook my head. "But this curfew sucks."

She gave a humorless laugh. "Not like my parents would let me go out anyway with the wolves last night."

"Wolves?" I asked carefully.

She walked closer to the fence. "Didn't you hear them? They were howling all over the neighborhood."

"I must have missed it. We were dropping off a friend." Before she could ask any more questions, I switched to the next subject I could think of. "I didn't see you at school today."

She shrugged. "Yeah, my parents made me go to Council with them."

"A council about what?"

She sighed. "The wolves again. The Council's convinced that they've overgrown the city." Her tone sounded strange, like she wasn't sure how she felt about the wolves herself. I wondered if she knew that Chet was one of them.

"Sounds like a strange problem for a big city. Why don't they just get someone to shoot them?" My gut clenched at the question, but I knew it was something a regular outsider would ask.

I could see her frown in the moonlight. "Who says they're the ones that have to leave?"

Her question caught me by surprise, but caution outweighed my curiosity about her opinion. The talk about wolves, the fight today, and the empty house behind me was too much to take at the moment. I made my way past the punching bag to the back fence.

"Where are you going?" she asked in surprise.

"Out."

"Out?" She followed me on her side of the fence. "You can't go out; there's a curfew."

Exasperated, I turned and faced her through the wooden slats. "Look, my mom's at her job, no one's home, and I'm fed up with being by myself. There's got to be something to do here at night." I grabbed the panel that ran along the back of the fence and levered myself over the top to drop in the alley behind it.

"You're crazy," she said, but I heard her struggle to get over as well. She landed beside me a few seconds later, a gleam of triumph in her eyes.

"I'm Jaze."

"Nicole," she said with a beautiful smile. "But everyone calls me Nikki." She combed her long black hair back with her fingers and tied it in a ponytail with a rubber band she pulled from her pocket. "Alright, I'm ready."

"For what?"

She grinned. "Anything; bring it on. After what I saw today, I don't doubt you have more trouble up your sleeves."

I stared at her. "I thought you weren't at school."

She laughed and held up her phone. "I got five different views of the fight, five. Keep it up and you'll be the best

54

known delinquent in the city."

I shoved my hands in my pockets and started down the alley. She waited for a minute, then ran to catch up.

"Boy, you're touchy. I figured a guy who'd mess with Chet would have a thick hide."

"He'd have to," I said. I watched her out of the corner of my eye, but she shrugged it off and looked into the yards we passed.

"This is exciting," she said in a loud whisper.

"You've never been out in the city at night?" I asked incredulously.

"Not when it's against the law!" I laughed and she slapped my shoulder. "Shhh, do you want us to get caught?"

I grinned and shook my head, catching the enthusiasm that shone on her face. We made our way behind a grocery store, through the parking lot of an abandoned gas station, and into the next alley. Adrenaline began to course through my veins at the thrill of the night hunt, the escape from society, and the cool breeze that brought with it a promise of rain that smelled so sweet it was all I could do to keep from standing still and just taking it all in.

It wasn't until we reached the back of a run-down mall that someone spotted us.

"Hey you two!" a security guard sporting a reflective orange vest and a nightstick shouted at us.

Nikki and I looked at each other. "Run!" I shouted. She grabbed my hand and we dashed across the sparsely lit parking lot toward the skeletal outlines of partly-constructed houses beyond.

I could have run faster, but I didn't want to leave Nikki to the whims of the guard. Luckily, he stopped at the edge of the parking lot and waved his stick at us.

"Whoa, give a guy an inch," I said when we'd caught our breath. We made our way between the houses. The frames made silhouettes like dinosaur bone shadows along the freshly paved road.

"Yeah, seriously," Nikki replied. "There's a man on a power trip." She must have realized that she was still holding my hand because she let it go and gave me a self-conscious smile.

"Do you think he would have run away if we turned around and started chasing him?"

She laughed. "Probably. We'll have to remember to bring our own orange vests next time, then we'll see who's tough."

The thought made me chuckle. "You'd be pretty intimidating in orange. I don't think it'd be fair to him."

She was about to reply when a yell caught my attention. "Wait," I held up a hand. "Do you hear that?" Another yell sounded, followed by a shout of triumph.

"What?" Nikki asked.

I hurried toward the sound, afraid that someone might be in trouble. She followed close behind.

We ran across two vacant roads, through a bingo hall parking lot, and jumped over a ditch. A fence about eight feet high stretched off into the night, and beyond it I could see a dozen smaller roofs. Yelling followed by cheers came again from behind it. "What is this place?"

"It's a giant swap meet on the weekends. I didn't think anyone came here during the week." She peered through the fence, but the only thing we could see was the back of a building.

I laced my fingers together. "I'll give you a hand."

She stared at me. "What? No way. I'm not going in there."

I pointed toward the sound. "Listen. There's no screaming, just laughing and yelling. Sounds like a bunch of people having a good time. I just want to see what they're doing." I gave her a smile. "It'll take two seconds. We'll just peek in, see what's up, and then leave."

She gave me a suspicious glance. "You promise?"

I nodded and put my hands together again. She sighed, then stepped onto them. She let out a tiny squeak when I hoisted her to the top of the fence, but she grabbed the top pole, levered herself over, then lowered until she could fall to the ground. "But how are you-"

I jumped and caught the bar with my hands, then pulled myself over and landed on the ground beside her.

"Oh." She bent to tie a shoelace. I waited impatiently until she stood. "Ok, I'm ready," she whispered.

I led the way around the back of the first building, across a gravel pathway, then along a second. The noise grew louder as we neared the center of the complex. We passed rows of sheds with rolling doors pulled down and locked. The scents of old books, furniture, tires, animal cages, clothes, cheap electronics, stale food, and garbage filled my nose. By the smell of things, the place was very active on the weekends.

We edged along the last row of sheds and peered out.

A group of about twenty high schoolers flew by on roller skates chasing a green puck.

"What the-" Nikki grabbed my shirt and pulled me back when they came racing back in the other direction.

"Street hockey?" she asked, the surprise on her face identical to mine.

"Why not, I guess?" I said. I stepped back around the corner and she followed close behind with a hesitant hand on my arm.

A group of skaters shoved a member of the other team into a stack of garbage cans. He floundered for a moment through the trash, then rose with the puck in hand and a triumphant grin on his face. Someone hit it out of his grasp, he yelled back, and they raced off again.

"No picking up the puck!" a kid shouted, skating by.

"It was in the garbage can," the first boy protested, following close behind. They argued as they made a mad dash toward the other side where they barely missed a football flying through the air.

Several students ran after the football and a brawl ensued when they reached it. Two older students stood on the sidelines arguing about whose ball it was. They didn't seem at all phased when another student kicked a soccer ball in their direction. They threw it back and the student hit it with his knee to two students waiting at the far end.

I was surprised at how many students watched the games from the sides, jumping clear when any ball or the puck came at them. Girls and boys lounged on benches that had been pulled out at the other end of the clearing. Several students sat in a circle around a manhole cover and tossed cards onto a pile. Nikki caught up to me as I walked through the crowd. Both of us tried to act like we fit in. I didn't catch a single whiff of werewolf and began to relax.

"So this is what a bunch of oppressed high school students do during curfew," I said to her.

Her eyes were wide. "I guess so; I never knew!"

The skaters rushed by again; we dodged them and made our way to the benches. "I know one thing," I told her.

"What's that?"

"I've gotta unpack my skates."

She stared at me. "You're going to play with them?"

She made it sound like I wanted to take on a whole S.W.A.T. team by myself.

"Why not?"

"You could get killed!" she replied.

I gave a grim smile. "Oh, and that would be any different from my life right now?"

She was silent for a few minutes, then surprised me when she said, "Well, if you're going to play, I am too."

It was my turn to stare. "You, out there?"

We both turned to look just as the entire north team crashed into the goalie of the south team and flattened him against a park bench that had been flipped on its side to serve as a goal. They helped each other up, one picked up the puck and threw it, and they were off again.

"It could be fun." She grinned. "Besides, there are girls out there. And girls can be more aggressive than boys."

"Oh really."

"Yes, really."

I laughed and shrugged. "Fine, if you want to play, meet me behind the fence tomorrow night with some skates."

A boy tapped my shoulder. "You guys wanna drink?" He held out a selection of sodas.

"Thanks." I took a Pepsi.

Nikki took a Sprite. "Who do we pay?" she asked.

The boy shrugged. "No one; it's covered by the school, right Bode?" he shouted over his shoulder.

A husky guy who looked like he could take on a bull single-handedly raised a can in salute. The coolers he leaned against looked overloaded with cans.

"That's the quarterback of the high school football team," Nikki whispered to me in surprise. We raised our sodas back and he gave us a thumbs-up.

"So, what do they do if the cops show up?" Nikki asked the boy who gave us the drinks.

He pointed to two students I hadn't noticed perched on top of the back buildings. I saw two more at the other two corners of the square. "We take turns acting as sentries for a night. If the cops show up, we're outta here before they know anything's up."

He left and I turned back to Nikki. "The things you would've missed if I hadn't shown up next door."

"Hey, it's the brawler!" someone shouted.

I shook my head, but several students came over anyway. "You took on like twenty guys by yourself," one boy said.

"Yeah, and you didn't even bleed!" another crowed.

Embarrassed, I shrugged. "They got me, but I'll live."

"Show us," an overzealous girl with red streaks in her hair demanded.

"You got hurt?" Nikki asked quietly next to me.

"It's nothing, really," I protested. I lifted up my shirt so that they could see my side, forgetting that the wound had opened again when I punched the bag. Dried blood caked it, making it look worse than it was.

Several students gasped and whistled. Nikki touched my arm. "You should have that looked at," she said.

I shook my head and lowered my shirt. "I'm fine; it's really not that bad."

"And you gave them worse than that!" a skinny redhead from the group said.

A student with short black dreadlocks grinned. "Dude, those guys have beaten up practically every kid in school; it's good to see someone get the best of them for once."

"Yeah," other students agreed.

I shrugged. "Hey, I'm just glad to find a place to escape this curfew."

Several students laughed. The dreadlocked guy held out his fist. "You're more than welcome."

I bumped his knuckles with my own. "Thanks."

Nikki grabbed my arm after they drifted away. "Chet's gang normally doesn't fight with knives. He's not that way." Her eyes were serious, pleading for me to believe her.

I shrugged. "Maybe someone dropped it and I rolled on it." I swallowed my sarcastic tone at the worried look in her eyes. "Don't worry, I'm not going to get them in trouble or anything. Besides, the Principal seems to think there's something funny about them anyway."

This time, her eyes tightened at the corners and she looked away. "They can be dangerous, Jaze. You need to stay away from them."

"Why? What's so dangerous about them?" She stared at me, and I thought for a minute that she was going to confess, but then someone yelled, 'head's up', and we both ducked to avoid the puck that flew past.

After the mad scramble of hockey players passed, Nikki looked down at her watch. "I've got to get home before my parents miss me."

"Your parents miss you?" I asked.

She slapped my shoulder and pulled me to my feet. "Come on," she said.

I shook my head, shoving my hands in my pockets. "Fine, I wouldn't want your parents thinking you'd been kidnapped or whatever the curfew is supposed to prevent."

She grinned at me and walked past the tables. We said goodbye to a few of the students and promised to return the next evening. My heart slowed when one of them mentioned that they would be there every night but on a full moon.

The walk home was quiet and uneventful. There was no sign of the security guard when we crossed the parking lot. The stars lit our path and gave a friendly hue to the midnight shadows. Nikki and I climbed our fences and said quiet goodbyes.

I entered my empty house and sat on the couch, thinking about Chet and his gang. There was something there, something that wasn't quite right, but I couldn't put a finger on it. I finally gave up and went to bed, leaving on a few lights for Mom.

Chapter 8

"I need your help with something," I told Brock on the way to school the next morning.

His face lit up. "Anything, man. Just name it!"

A car passed us slowly, its windows tinted too dark to see through. I watched until it turned the corner ahead of us and drove out of sight. "I need to see some of the student files."

Brock glanced at me, his expression curious. "Sure. The Administrators have a meeting right after school and I told them I'd watch the front desk. That'd be a good time."

"Perfect," I replied distractedly. My attention was on the car again. It had circled the block and then pulled to a stop at the curb on our side of the street not far ahead.

"They leave me the keys and it'll be no problem. . ." he noticed I wasn't paying attention and followed my gaze. "Jaze, what's up?"

"That car." The passenger side door opened and a man of medium build wearing a faded jean jacket and a black baseball hat got out. My heart slowed. "Brock, we've got to find another way to school."

I looked around, wondering if it was too late for Brock to hide. Maybe he could go ahead and pretend he wasn't with me. I discarded the idea as quickly as it came. It was too dangerous if they had already linked us together. The other occupants stayed in the car, but I could see silhouettes of the driver and two more men in the back seat. I fought to keep my breathing even.

The man in the baseball hat turned. We were close enough to see the smile he gave that showed too many teeth. A breeze brushed past him to us and I fought down the urge to growl.

"Jaze, how fortunate to meet you here!" he said. His

tone was casual, but his eyes studied me intently.

"Uncle Mason, what are you doing here?" I forced the words out lightly despite the knot in my throat. It was all I could do to keep my face expressionless, let alone look happy to see him.

"I just thought I'd check to make sure you and your mother got moved in okay." I had to fight to keep my fists unclenched when he mentioned her, but he didn't seem to notice. "I heard you were here and figured you might need a hand." He gave a shrug. "It's the least I can do, after what happened to my brother."

I ground my teeth so hard at the mention of Dad I was surprised they didn't break. I stopped a few feet from him so I wouldn't give in to the impulse to throw him through the windshield of his car. "We're doing fine, thank you. Brock and I are late for school, so we've gotta go."

"Oh, I understand." He turned his sickly sweet smile on my friend. "Brock, is it?" I kicked myself mentally for giving Mason his name. When Brock nodded, his eyes alternating between Mason and me, Mason smiled again. "A pleasure to meet you, my boy."

Brock glanced at me. "Thanks." It sounded more like a question than a response.

I grabbed Brock's arm. "Come on, we're going to be late."

Brock followed close behind; I passed the car facing it until I practically walked backwards. "Thanks for stopping by, Uncle Mason. I'll be sure to tell Mom you send your regards."

He nodded. "You do that. I went by the house, but she must still be at work. Let her know I hope she's settled in comfortably at the office."

Cold fire ran through my veins, but I forced myself to turn and continued to school. We passed through the doors just as the first bell rang. I threw my plated silver bracelet into a cup, stepped through the metal detector, and put it back on in a blur, angry and more frustrated than I could think. My feet took me toward my classroom and it wasn't until Brock called my name the third time that it registered.

"Jaze!" His face was red and he fought to catch his breath as he put on the last few pieces of silver jewelry he had taken off for the metal detectors.

I waited for him. "Sorry. I was distracted."

"Tell me about it!" At the look on my face, Brock slowed down. "Was that who I think it was?"

I nodded.

"What's he doing here? I mean, I assume you guys moved to get away from him or something if he's the one you told me about that-"

I held up a hand to cut him off. "Don't say it. I can't handle it right now."

Brock nodded quickly. "Okay, no prob. But what do we do?"

We had reached my classroom. I glanced inside, wanting more than anything to go check on Mom and not sit inside a brick room all day listening to lectures that wouldn't sink in past the tornado of thoughts in my head anyway. "I don't know." I took a deep breath to slow my pounding heart. "But until I figure it out, we've got to go on as normal."

Brock nodded, his eyes wide.

I gestured to the classroom. "I've gotta go. See you at lunch."

I slid into an empty seat just before the second bell rang. Two more students ran in late and received a reprimand from the teacher. Mason wasn't supposed to know we were here. We had justified using my real name because we needed my school records for the transfer, but I didn't think he would track us so quickly. He obvious had more pull than I realized. But to take a trip so far east just to check on us? He either worried I suspected something or was here on business of his own.

I wondered if I had given anything away. We had never had a close relationship anyway, so I hoped the standoffish encounter didn't give him any reason to suspect I knew anything. I forced myself to stay seated, rationalizing that Mom would be safest at work surrounded by her coworkers and customers. Something was definitely wrong and I had to get to the bottom of it soon for all our sakes.

***

The rest of the day passed without incident beside a few accusatory stares and the occasional jostle in the hallway from Chet's gang. By the time Brock and I were alone in the office, I was so tense my muscles shook.

Brock glanced down the hall toward the teachers' lounge where they held their meeting. He looked as stressed as I felt. "Amazed we didn't get jumped again?" he asked. He pulled the office door shut and locked it.

"The day isn't over yet," I replied grimly. I studied both the long halls visible from the office, but they were empty. I shook my head. "Let's get this over with."

I followed him past the desks toward Principal Stewart's office; we stopped at a door on the left side of the hall just before it. The keys jangled more than necessary in Brock's hand, and I glanced over to see him bite his lip. "Nervous?" I asked quietly.

He grinned and shook his head. "Excited, actually. I never thought to look in the student files for evidence about the werewolves. Now's my chance!"

I shook my head, not sure we would find anything helpful. Brock opened the door and flipped on the light. Neon hummed above, illuminating a tiny room with four filing cabinets across the left wall and the same on the right. A short table sat at the far end already piled with files. Brock went straight to the third cabinet on the left. "These are the Junior files."

"What about those over there?" I asked, gesturing to the opposite row.

"Those are students who have already graduated." He paused, a hand on the cabinet door. "Do you think we should check those, too?"

I debated, then shook my head. "We don't have time. Let's just pull files on Chet's gang and go from there."

He started pulling files alphabetically from the drawer. When he turned to set a few on the table, I grabbed Mouse's out and slipped it behind the ones I held. I fought back a wry smile. Mouse's real name, Nicky Strouse, left little to the imagination as to how he had gotten his nickname.

I settled on the floor with my back against a filing cabinet and flipped through Chet's file. Brock leaned against the table and did the same. We both searched silently through the files for several minutes. I was amazed at how many warnings and detentions Chet had received. But as far as I could tell, he had never been suspended.

"Um," Brock broke the silence a few minutes later. "What exactly are we looking for?"

I shrugged. "Not sure, but I'm hoping I'll know when we find it."

Brock turned back to his file and muttered, "Very helpful."

I fought back a grin and grabbed another file. Two pages in, I stopped. I read the single sentence typed on a plain white sheet of paper and my heart slowed. I grabbed Chet's file, found a similar sheet in his, then dropped it and grabbed another file. Four pages in, I found the same thing. I dropped all the files and leaned back against the metal cabinet; bile rose in my throat.

"Jaze, what's wrong?" Brock leaned toward me, his eyes bright with concern.

I closed my eyes and rubbed them hard, willing the pages in the files to disappear. Only I knew they wouldn't. It made too much sense. "I found what we're looking for."

Brock's eyebrows lifted. "Really? You look like you found a ghost or something."

"Might as well have," I muttered. At his look, I opened Chet's file and pointed at the page. "Read this."

Brock took it and cleared his throat. "Parents killed in car accident Sophomore year."

"And this." I handed him one of the others I had found.

"Mother died in house fire, Freshman year."

Wordlessly, I handed him another.

His voice grew quieter. "Father, Mother, and older brother killed in car accident, Sophomore year." He looked up at me. "Jaze, what is this?"

"There's one in every file I've looked at." My throat tightened, but I forced out the words, "Including my own."

Brock stared at me as the implication hit him. "You mean someone is killing the werewolves?"

"The adult werewolves," I clarified.

"Why would they do that?"

My voice dropped as I fought to control the anger. "Someone is killing off the older, stronger wolves. That way, they can be in charge. And I have an idea just who that might be," I concluded with a growl.

"Your uncle."

I nodded and rose to my feet, jamming the papers back into the files I held. "We've got to stop him."

Brock took the files before I could mangle them too badly and proceeded to put them back in the cabinets. "If he's killing off the stronger werewolves, then he's got two alphas left here." He glanced at me. "Do you think he'll try to kill you next?"

"He's already tried."

"When?" Brock asked in surprise.

"Remember the knives when we were attacked in the hall? Silver knives are one of Mason's call signs."

Brock frowned. "But aren't there werewolf laws against this sort of thing? Something to stop one werewolf from becoming too powerful?"

I nodded numbly. "There are Elders who enforce the laws. They should be handling this. I don't know why someone hasn't noticed that all of the Alphas are being systematically killed off." Rage filled me so intensely that I couldn't contain it anymore. I left the room before I damaged anything.

"Where are you going?" Brock yelled down the hall.

"Home. I've got some things I've gotta do," I shouted over my shoulder. I turned the deadbolt and shoved through the glass doors that led out of the office.

Brock ran after me and stopped at the doors. "Be careful, Jaze!"

I hesitated and turned. "You have a safe way home?"

He nodded. "Mom was planning to pick me up. Clothes shopping or something like that." He shuddered. "Looking forward to it."

I nodded. "Okay, be safe. I'll meet you tomorrow at your place." I turned and jogged down the street, glancing back once to make sure that Brock locked himself safely back in the school.

***

When I reached our house, I went straight to my room and pulled out the chest with Dad's belongings. Until that point, I hadn't truly wanted to believe that Uncle Mason, my father's own brother, was the one who had killed him. But in light of what I had found, and with Mason showing up today, it was undeniable. I pulled the leather jacket up to my face and took a deep breath. Dad's scent, the wild warm smell of the woods, the hunt, and a touch of Mom's flowery perfume surrounded me. I closed my eyes tight against the tears that spilled down my cheeks.

He had been a good dad, the best a boy could ask for. He had taken me to little league games, taught me how to fish, catch, camp, and the intricacies involved in werewolf life. With him, nothing had seemed impossible. Now, everything did. I thought of Mom, the way she tried to hold everything together by moving us to this new place. How would she feel if she knew Mason had been the one to give Dad up to the Hunters, and that he knew where we were now? I wouldn't run again, but she wasn't safe.

I leaned against the bed, the jacket across my knees.

"What would you do, Dad?" I whispered past the knot in my throat. There were too many people here who would be hurt if I left. Chet, for all his bravado and hostility, had a pack to take care of, a pack that would be turned over to Mason if my uncle got rid of him. Then I thought of Nikki. What if she was there when Mason went after Chet? I had to warn her. But how?

I put the jacket back in the chest, looked at Dad's few remaining belongings one last time, then shut it and pushed it back under the bed. I surveyed the cardboard boxes around my room, then opened the first one with the old computer Mom had given me.

***

My muscles tensed when the front door opened. "Hey kiddo, I'm home," Mom called. The door shut and she made her way to the kitchen followed by the sound of plastic bags and a few paper ones dumped on the table. The scent of orange chicken and rice wafted up the stairs. My stomach growled and I followed it down to the kitchen.

"I brought Chinese," Mom said in a muffled voice, her head buried in the refrigerator. She then looked back at me with a warm smile. "But I guess you already knew that."

I laughed. "The nose knows." We repeated Dad's favorite saying at the same time, then stopped and looked at each other. I couldn't take the sadness in Mom's eyes, the rush of memories and the knowledge of what was taken away from us. Anger at Mason came so quickly it stole my breath and I had to look away for a moment, afraid of what she would see on my face. I took a breath and forced a laugh as I turned back. "Dad always said I could smell food from a mile away."

Mom laughed too, tiny laugh lines at the corners of her eyes. "And he could smell it from two." She rose to her feet with a sigh. "I keep pretending he's away on a business trip or something; that one of these days he'll come through the door with a vase of daisies."

I nodded. Though my heart protested, I gave in to the urge to talk about him. "I dream about him sometimes, about running through the forest as wolves, and of the first time he took us to the lake. Do you remember that?"

Mom laughed. "He was like a little kid at Disneyland. That was when he taught you how to track. You couldn't have been more than eight or nine."

"Seven," I remembered. "He kept saying seven was magical because that's when werewolves turn into wolves for the first time."

"He was so proud when he found out you were an Alpha," Mom said. She reached over and fondled my dark blond hair. "Who would've thought?"

"I still wonder why. You're not a werewolf. At the most, I should have been a gray."

Mom nodded. "Our little miracle."

I had stopped believing in miracles, but didn't say so. I threw out my next thought. "I worry about you all by yourself, Mom. Do you want to visit Aunt Sam or something?"

She looked at me in surprise. "And leave you here by yourself? There's no way I could do that."

"I'd be okay, I've got friends at school, and Brock could stay over."

She shook her head, already protesting. "No, I don't want to leave you alone, especially not now. The full moon's coming up and you shouldn't be alone."

I grimaced. "I have a week. It'll be okay."

She shook her head again with the stubborn look on her face that said she wasn't going to budge. "I'm not leaving you, and that's the end of the discussion. There's too much going on right now and I can't leave my job anyway."

But the way she said it left a slight hope that I might be able to make it work if I handled it correctly. I dropped the subject as quick as I could. "Okay, no problem. I just worry about you, that's all."

She set some paper plates on the table and smiled at me. "Worry about me? I'm the parent, I should be worrying about you, and I do."

"I'm fine, really. Everything's going great at school." I had never been a very good liar, but luckily she was occupied with setting out the food and didn't notice.

"I'm glad to hear it." She handed me a pair of chopsticks and I took the seat across from her. We both glanced at the empty chair that would have been Dad's.

"He wanted what was best for us. He'd want us to be happy," she said quietly.

I nodded. "We will be." I hoped I sounded more positive than I felt.

I must have because she grabbed my hand across the table and gave it a squeeze. "Thank you."

"For what?"

"For being the best son a mother could ask for," she replied. Tears glistened in her eyes.

I shook my head. "Mom-"

"No," she replied firmly, "I'm serious. You've just gone through something no boy ever should, and you've handled it so maturely. Losing your dad, going to a new school, starting a new life. I've had to work and I haven't been there for you like I should. It hasn't been easy, but you haven't made it harder."

I blinked back tears at the pain in her voice. "It's okay, Mom. We're going to be okay."

She smiled at me and gave my hand one last squeeze. Then she sat back and wiped her tears away. "You're right. We are going to be okay." She smiled down at her food and attempted to set her chopsticks in her hand correctly so she could use them to eat. They kept slipping until she finally tossed them on the table and grabbed a fork. "I never could get those right," she laughed.

I waved the chicken I held firmly in my own chopsticks and she threw a fortune cookie at me. "Show off!"

Chapter 9

I grabbed my skates by the back door and pushed it open.

"Wait," Mom called from the living room.

I turned reluctantly. "Yeah?"

She appeared in the kitchen doorway. "You going out? Isn't there a curfew or something?"

I shrugged. "Just to keep the kids out of trouble. You know me, I'll be good." I fought back a smile.

She caught sight of the skates and her eyebrows rose. "You're going roller skating? You haven't worn those things for years."

"I have some friends I'm meeting up with."

She looked skeptical, but finally shrugged. "Okay, just don't get in trouble. I don't want to get on a first name basis with the sheriff like our last town."

I grinned and pushed open the sliding door. She sighed and returned to her book on the couch.

"Your mom worries?" Nikki asked from the darkness of the yard next door.

I tossed the skates over the back fence and jumped over after them. "I've had kind-of what you might call a troubled history."

She climbed over the fence and gave me a teasing smile. "Oh, a rebel, huh? My dad warned me to stay away from those."

I glanced at her. "So what are you doing out here?"

She smiled, her eyes catching the starlight. "Being rebellious."

I glanced at her skates. She had tied the laces together and hung them over her shoulder. They were bright neon pink and sparkled with glitter. I lifted an eyebrow.

She pushed my shoulder. "I got them when I was going through a pink phase. All little girls go through it."

I laughed. "How long ago was that, last year?"
She shook her head. "We better get going, rebel, or we'll miss out on the fun."

We jogged down the aisle between the fences.

"Wow," I said after a few minutes.

She frowned. "What?"

"You must have had thumper feet to fit in those when you were younger."

I laughed when she shoved me. "My parents bought them big so they wouldn't have to buy a new pair when I grew out of them."

"I guess they thought the pink phase would last a while."

She grabbed my roller skates before I could protest. "Let's see what we can learn from your little skates, shall we?" She slowed to a walk as she looked them over. "Geesh, you don't take care of your stuff."

I glanced at the deep grooves cut in the sides, the scuffed toes and holes where the brake screws should be. "Let's just say these have seen a lot of botched dares over their time."

"No brakes?" she asked skeptically.

"They get in the way," I replied with a grin.

She shook her head and handed them back.

We walked along in amiable silence until we reached the mall parking lot. We waited a few minutes and, sure enough, along came the security guard swinging his nightstick as he moseyed between the few street lamps that still worked.

Nikki bent down and took off her shoes.

"What are you doing?" I whispered.

"Having a little fun," she replied. She looked pointedly at my skates. "Care to join me?"

76

I watched her silently as I took off my shoes, tied the laces together and hung them over one shoulder, then pulled on my skates.

Nikki took off before I was finished. She skated slowly across the parking lot, weaving between the circles of light around the street lamps that hadn't burned out yet. She got surprisingly close to the security guard before he noticed her.

"Hey, you!" he shouted. He ran toward her with his nightstick raised. I didn't think he meant to hit her with it, but adrenaline rushed through my veins just the same and I finished tying my skates with a growl.

Nikki just laughed and skated backwards out of his reach. "Just wanted to say hi," she said sweetly.

"You know there's a curfew!" he huffed as he fought to keep up with her.

"Is it to keep us safe, or you?" she asked, her eyes glittering as she teased him. She let him get closer and he waved his nightstick menacingly.

"To keep us from the werewolves," the guard growled. He swiped the stick at her sword-like and she jumped back just in time, her eyes widening slightly.

I crouched to increase my speed and my wheels hummed like angry hornets over the pavement. I reached out and grabbed the nightstick before he could make another attempt to catch her. He let go in surprise and I spun to a halt a few steps away.

"What do you mean, to keep us from the werewolves?" I pressed, my heart racing.

He held out his hand and glared at me, his chest heaving as he fought to catch his breath. He looked mad, but there was a light in his eyes like he secretly enjoyed a bit of a tussle after all the lonely nights on the job.

I shook my head. "Uh-uh. Not until you talk to us." I twirled the nightstick experimentally. It was weighted well and moved smoothly in my hands.

He shrugged and bent over with his hands on his knees. "You kids shouldn't be out here. It's dangerous. Why do you think I patrol?"

"You're bored?" Nikki put in helpfully.

"You like adventure?" I added, glancing around pointedly at the very empty lot.

"You're afraid someone will steal the light bulbs?" Nikki looked up at the lamp closest to us, a baleful gray pole with a missing light. "You're not doing a very good job."

The security guard cracked a smile. "Nice try. I do it because the curfew's set for a reason. Things happen here that you don't want to know about."

"We do want to know," I pressed. I glanced at Nikki, hoping this could lead us into a conversation later about her dangerous werewolf boyfriend.

The guard held out his hand again. I hesitated, then handed him the nightstick with a flourish. "Your sword, sir knight," Nikki supplied. I bowed and she giggled when the guard took the stick back.

"Yes, well, hmph," he muttered, shoving it back into his belt. Then he glanced back at us. "I shouldn't be telling you these things. It's really against the rules."

I shrugged. "Well, we're breaking the rules anyway, so we might as well know why they're there in the first place."

Nikki nodded, her long black hair swaying. "We might be more inclined to follow them if we knew what they were for."

The guard regarded us silently for a moment, then sighed. "Very well." He glanced around as though afraid someone might be spying in the middle of the huge empty parking lot. He stepped closer and lowered his voice. "There're werewolves in this town, and I suspect more than the city knows how to deal with."

"Werewolves?" I forced a skeptical tone.

He nodded. "I've seen 'em."

Nikki and I glanced at each other. Her eyes were wide.

The guard continued. "No normal wolf is that big. These werewolves are bigger than Great Danes and have bright golden eyes that reflect the moon." He warmed up to the telling, his voice lifting. "They run in packs, huge packs, and howl the likes of which makes my blood run ice cold in my veins. They came right through here, and the lamps went out as they ran by." He leaned closer to Nikki, his expression dramatically horrified. "One of 'em stopped and looked me straight in the eyes. He licked his big chops and grinned like he was laughing at me, then he turned and ran off with the rest of 'em."

I fought back a smile at his scare tactics. "Then we'd better get outta here, huh?"

He nodded. "I'd recommend it. That curfew's in place for a reason. The city's scared and they don't know what to do about it. So they hide the people and let the werewolves run wild."

I shrugged. "Sounds reasonable." He and Nikki both stared at me and I rolled back a couple of inches on my skates. I rushed on, "Well, if they're as dangerous as you say, it'd be good to avoid them."

The security guard nodded in agreement. "Exactly what I'm saying. It's not safe for you kids to be roaming around here with who knows what other creatures lurking in the night."

Nikki smiled. "We'll take that into consideration. Thank you, Mr. . ."

"Sathing, Charlie Sathing." He stuck out his hand and she shook it.

I followed. "I'm Jaze and this is Nikki. It's good to meet you, Mr. Sathing. We'll watch out for the werewolves," I said as lightly as I could.

"You do that," he replied with a satisfied nod.

We turned and skating slowly across the parking lot and into the shadows beyond. We stopped and switched back to our shoes on the dead brown grass.

"He's a nice guy," Nikki said, a touch of surprise in her voice.

I nodded. "Very nice. I thought he was going to hit you with his club!"

"Me, too!" She laughed, "I guess people aren't always what they seem."

A chill ran through me and I nodded in wordless reply, wondering what she would think if she knew my secret.

"Well," she said, oblivious of my train of thought. "Let's get going before we miss out."

"Right," I agreed.

We walked through the darkness to the fence and the sounds of voices beyond. I linked my hands together and Nikki grinned at me. "Good thing you moved next door, rebel boy. Things were starting to get boring."

"Never a dull moment in my life," I said. Luckily, she didn't catch the bitterness of my tone; I hefted her over the fence and then jumped up after her.

We stopped at the main junction between the aisles just in time to avoid the oncoming puck and a pack of roller skaters inches behind. A scrawny kid in the front tripped on a rock, the one behind fell over him, and suddenly the whole group lay in a massive laughing heap on the cement. Nikki and I sat to lace up our skates.

"Hey," the scrawny kid said, pushing back his scratched up helmet. "More players!"

"Yeah," a few others shouted as they fought to untangle themselves from the pile.

An older student dressed in black from head to toe skated over and handed us a couple of sticks and two strips of cloth. "Nice to have ya. Just jump in on the blue team. They're short a few today."

"Uh," Nikki said, taking the cloth. "Are there any rules we need to know about?"

Several students still sprawled on the pavement laughed. The older student shook his head. "Just don't go crying home to mommy if you get hurt." He smiled, but there was a hint of steel behind his words.

"We'll be fine," I said. I took the sticks from his hands.

He looked at me closer. "Hey, aren't you the kid from that fight?" When I didn't deny it, he laughed. "Dang, guess I'll choose the blue team next time!" He skated off with a stick in hand and threw me one last look over his shoulder before joining the fray.

I glanced at Nikki and shrugged. She smiled and tied the blue cloth around my arm.

"Come on, they don't wait for anybody around here," one of the blue team members shouted.

I finished tying her band, tossed our shoes on a nearby pile, and gestured with my stick. "Ladies first."

"Thank you," she said.

My heart skipped a beat at the smile she gave me as she passed by. I stared after her, noticing the way the lights made purple highlights in her black hair. My attention was torn away when the puck raced back in my direction.

"Hey Romeo, gonna play?" someone shouted. I jumped in and hoped no one noticed my crimson face.

After a long hard game in which nobody kept score, Nikki and I relaxed on top of one of the long rows of selling stalls. The roofs were metal and still held some of the warmth of the sun that had long set. It helped ease the ache from my sore muscles.

We drank cold sodas and watched the few stars that made it through the light-polluted sky. The moon rested on the edge of the horizon, quietly observing its subjects. A week from today it would be full. My bones ached for the change while I dreaded it. A forced change in strange territory was not a good thing.

Now would be my best shot to break the news to Nikki that her boyfriend was a werewolf, and not just any wolf, the leader of the biggest pack I had ever seen that was about to be decimated by my power-crazy uncle so he could have the control for himself. I grimaced inwardly. There really wasn't ever a great time to tell someone that. I swallowed, searching for a delicate way to say it, when she spoke.

"So the security guard was sure interesting with his theory of werewolves," she said in a neutral tone.

I glanced at her. "About that," I started, but she cut me off.

"I need to tell you something." She sat up and looked at me, her expression guarded.

I sat up, too, and turned the soda can in my hands. The condensation pooled on my fingers and I wiped it on my knees. "Shoot."

"I've never told anyone," she said with a nervous laugh. "I didn't want them to think I was a freak or something."

I could understand that. "So why tell me?"

She gave me a soft smile that stole my breath. "You're different. You don't seem to care what anyone thinks, and you're not caught up in the petty stuff everyone seems to care about."

"Such as?" I prompted, curious.

"Oh, you know. Money, hair, clothes, that sort of thing."

I glanced down, wondering if that was a shot, and she grabbed my arm. "Not that that's bad," she said quickly. She smiled again, this time showing pretty white teeth. "It's refreshing. And I like your hair." She ran a hand through my tangled blond strands and a tremble ran through my body.

I closed my eyes for a second to compose myself, and when I opened them she was looking at me, her bright blue eyes large. "I've never met anyone like you. I feel like I could talk to you about anything. And we've only known each other for two days. Is that weird?"

I shook my head quickly. "No, not weird at all." I took a calming breath and spoke the truth. "I feel the same way about you." I felt exposed, vulnerable. It was the truth, but so much of the truth I wanted to take it back and pretend like I hadn't said anything. I needed my walls back up.

She smiled again, but this time her eyes sparkled too brightly. She blinked and tears caught on her lashes.

"Nikki, what wrong?" I asked, alarmed.

She shook her head and leaned against my shoulder, her head bowed on my chest. Her shoulders shook and I realized she was crying. I put an arm around her and held her, unsure of what else to do. An image of Mom's tears flashed in my mind. My heart clenched at the thought of her pain at losing Dad. I shut my eyes tight and forbade the echoing pain in my shredded heart to surface.

Nikki's silent sobs stopped eventually and she sniffed. She wiped her tears away with her hand and glanced up at me. "You must think I'm crazy," she said. Somehow, tear streaked cheeks made her look even more beautiful.

I shook my head. "Not at all." I gave a thoughtful frown. "I was wondering what there was that could make you so heartbroken, and who I needed to beat up to fix it."

It worked to make her smile. She shook her head with a breathless little laugh. "Not everything can be fixed by fighting, you know."

She laid back on the roof and I followed. She scooted closer and I moved my arm back so she could rest her head on my shoulder. We stared at the midnight sky as wisps of clouds chased the wind and twisted around the moon. My heart pounded at how close she was and I wondered if she could hear it.

A few minutes later, she sighed and turned her head away from me. "My parents are werewolf Hunters," she said so softly I barely heard her.

My heart slowed; ice replaced the blood in my veins. "What did you say?" I asked carefully.

She turned to look back at the sky. "My parents hunt werewolves. The security guard was right about them in this area. They're everywhere and my parents were sent here to find them."

I couldn't move. The implications sent steel into my bones. Adrenaline rushed to battle with the tiny window of peace I had found with Nikki. I shook my head in disbelief and she sat up.

"You don't believe me?" she asked.

I stared at her, not trusting myself to speak.

She gave a small smile. "I know, werewolves, right? It sounds so far fetched, like make believe. But they're real, Jaze. You've got to believe me. Mr. Sathing was right when he said the curfew was to keep people safe from them. Werewolves are vicious killers, and my parents are trying to find them before they can hurt anyone else."

I sat up slowly, avoiding her eyes as my mind raced. We lived next door to Hunters, the same blood-thirsty group of people who had killed my dad and many of the other werewolves I cared about. They were hunting right now, trying to find Chet's pack and wipe them out. Nikki was their daughter. I looked at her in disbelief.

"They're real," she repeated, mistaking my expression. "And that's all my parents care about." Tears sparkled in her eyes again, but she blinked them away. "Werewolves killed my older brother. They keep saying they're avenging him, but they never stop." She shook her head. "That's all they think about, the fact that the wolves killed Randy. They used to say they were only after the one who killed him, but they never found it, so they travel from city to city killing all that they can."

I fought to breathe past the knot that tightened in my stomach.

"I go home and that's all they talk about," she rushed on as though the words had been building up inside of her for so long she couldn't stop them. "They don't care about how school's going, about my boyfriend, or anything that goes on in my life."

I held very still, daring only to breathe as I fought to regain control of my emotions. I finally forced out, "So is that why you're with me?"

"What are you talking about?" she asked softly, her eyes searching mine.

"To get back at your parents? Is that why you're out here breaking the rules, hanging out with a *rebel?*" I hated the bitterness of my tone, but couldn't help it. Even the small shard of peace I had found on the roof had been stolen away by Hunters. I clenched my fists in my lap and fought not to hit something.

Nikki stared at me, her eyes bright with hurt. Then the expression turned to anger. "I told you I care about you, Jaze, and you think I'm seeking revenge on my parents or something?" She stood up on the roof, her own fists clenched. "I told you things nobody else knows about me. I trusted you. This doesn't have to be all about you. If you have your own reasons to sneak out at night, that's fine with me, but don't assume you know me."

She walked to the edge and lowered herself down on the far side.

"Nikki, wait," I said, my heart heavy as I climbed down after her.

She turned back, her eyes sparking. "Don't follow me. I don't want anything to do with you. You think you're so brave, that you can do whatever you want? Take your oh-so-composed self-confidence and shove it."

She stalked down the aisle and disappeared from sight. I stared after her, torn in so many directions I didn't know what to do. But I couldn't let her walk home in the middle of the night by herself with werewolves running around. I climbed slowly over the fence and waited in a dark corner near the front of the park for her to leave, then followed her home, careful to stay hidden. She glanced back once, and I suspected she knew I was following, but she turned away and walked to her house without looking again.

I leaned my forehead against her fence after she climbed it; her flowery scent lingered on the rough wood. She opened her back door, and then paused. "Thanks, Jaze, for ruining the one good night I've had since Randy died," she said quietly over her shoulder, then she went in and shut the door behind her.

The sound of her footsteps faded in the house and my heart stuttered. I shook my head against the wood, then turned my back to it and slid down against the fence. I bowed my head in my hands and hated myself for what I had said to Nikki, for the helplessness I felt in dealing with Mason, and most of all, for not being there when Dad needed my help. I might not have been able to save him, but he wouldn't have had to die alone.

A howl rose in the distance. I shut my eyes and ignored it, hoping that they would find me, that they would tear me apart and let me die the way I should have when Dad was killed. But then I thought of Mom finding my body the way we had found Dad's. I took a deep breath and pushed myself to my feet. I tossed the skates over the fence, climbed after them, and made my way slowly into the empty house that pretended to be a home.

Chapter 10

I couldn't shake my bad mood when Brock and I walked to school the next day. I went through the motion of attending class, but didn't hear a word the teachers said. Older, stronger werewolves were being killed, Mason had tracked us here, and now I had blown my friendship with Nikki because of who her parents were. She couldn't help what her parents did, and from what she told me last night, it sounded like she hated it anyway. But she didn't even glance my way in the lunchroom.

"So how do we tell the werewolves about why their parents died?" Brock asked as we walked slowly home.

I glanced at him, my train of thought interrupted. "Huh?"

He shrugged. "I assume that's why you haven't said a single word to me today. Just a lot on your mind."

I stopped and looked at him. He was right. Thinking back through the day, I hadn't spoken to him once. The last thing I needed to do was ignore the only friend I had left in the world. "I'm sorry, Brock. I didn't mean to." I sighed and shook my head. "I'm trying to figure some things out, but I shouldn't take it out on you. You've been a good friend."

He smiled and ducked his head in embarrassment. "Hey, you've got a lot going on, and you lost your dad. I have no idea what you're going through right now." He nodded to indicate our path. "This has been nice. With you, I don't have to worry about being bullied by Chet's gang on the way home."

"They used to bully you?" I asked, surprised.

"Well, more so when Mouse came with me. I don't think they like him very much."

I frowned, but wasn't surprised. Pack wolves don't get along too well with lone wolves. The little I had seen of

Mouse made me surprised that he had the guts to run alone. Maybe I needed to get to know him better.

"Why do you think-"

I held up a hand to cut Brock off. He dropped silent and the sirens sounded louder.

"What is it?" he asked, looking around nervously for danger.

"Sirens, heading this way."

"Like an ambulance?" He frowned, unsure why it bothered me.

I couldn't place my finger on it either, but as the sirens grew louder I heard the squeal of tires and horns honking. "Police sirens. You hear them?"

Brock nodded. "I do now."

I glanced down the road in the direction of the sirens and froze. Several elementary school age children crossed the street three blocks away. They giggled and several ran around the rest of the group holding someone's jacket in a game of keep away.

The sirens grew louder, followed by another squeal of tires. They were definitely headed that way. I threw off my backpack and ran down the road.

"Jaze, where are you-" Brock's voice cut off.

The cars rounded the corner several blocks from the children, bearing toward them at high speed. The children turned, their backs to me. Several screamed and a few ran across the road, but most of them didn't move.

A blue Honda with a ground kit sped toward the group. Its driver looked back at the cop cars following close behind. He didn't even seem to notice the kids.

"Run," I shouted at them, but they couldn't hear me over the sirens.

I pushed myself faster than I had ever run before.

The cars barreled down at us. One child hunched down in the middle of the road crying. Two of them started to run, but they weren't fast enough.

I dove in front of them a split second before the car. I turned my back just as the car hit me. The force knocked me to my knees and the car veered off into a tree on the left side of the road. I braced for the police cars, afraid they wouldn't stop in time. The screeching of brakes was followed by a crunch of metal as one of the cars in the back ran into one before it, but the car behind me stopped inches from us.

I glanced up at the children. They stared at me with wide eyes. The one who had crouched down looked up and his brown eyes met mine, then filled with tears. "It's okay," I told them. "You're okay."

I stood up slowly, wondering if I had broken anything. The adrenaline that pumped through my veins clouded any pain, but I knew I would feel it later. The police officers began climbing out of their cars, surprised and confused expressions on their faces. I needed to get out of there before they made me explain something unexplainable. I glanced at the children to make sure they were all alright, then started to walk back up the road.

"Hey you, wait!" someone called behind me.

I started to run.

"Hey, stop him!" the same person yelled.

I glanced up the road to check on Brock and was glad to see that he had disappeared. I ran down the closest unfenced yard, jumped over the back fence, and took off down the alley. By the time the officer jumped the fence, I was out of sight.

Brock waited on my front porch; his eyes widened with relief when I turned the corner. "I thought they killed you!" He exclaimed. "You got hit, then the car glanced off you and into a tree! How'd that happen?"

I gave him a wry smile and unlocked the door. "Werewolves in general are a lot stronger than humans, and Alphas are the strongest of the werewolves."

"So you knew you could stop it?" he asked when I pushed open the door.

I shook my head. "No idea, but I hoped." I stepped aside to let him go in. He stared at me for a moment, then shook his head and entered the house.

"Are you sure you're not going to, like, die or something from the impact? That car was going pretty fast."

I shook my head. "I think I'm fine. The driver was drunk; I could smell the alcohol when he hit."

Brock shook his head again. "And you had time to process that before the cops tried to run you over?"

I laughed. "They didn't try to run me over. They stopped, luckily. I don't know if I could have handled more than one of those." I lifted up my shirt and twisted in an attempt to look at my back in the living room mirror. "How bad is it?"

Brock turned to look and whistled. "Bad enough that I'm glad I'm not you."

Bruises already the color of blackberry jelly covered my back from just below my shoulders down to my pants. It probably went lower, but I wasn't about to check in front of Brock. I took an experimental breath and was surprised to find only mild pain in my ribs and back.

"Good thing werewolves heal quickly," I muttered under my breath. I pulled my shirt down and threw myself on the couch, then winced and sat up gingerly. "So," I said, "We need to tell Chet that Mason's the one who killed his parents."

Brock sighed. "From one job to the next, huh?"

"All in the line of duty for a werewolf," I replied.

He grinned. "Got anything to eat?"

***

That night was another of Mom's late nights at work. I felt bad that she worked so hard to support us, but was also relieved because it kept her out of Mason's way for a while. After Brock's mom picked him up, I called Mom's sister, Samantha.

"Hey darling, good to hear your voice. Did you guys get all moved in okay?"

"Yeah, mostly."

She laughed, and it was good to hear. Aunt Samantha and my mom were only a year apart, and sometimes they reminded me so much of each other it was like they were twins. Samantha was the only one that knew Mom had married a werewolf. And she got credit for supporting Mom in her decision. Aunt Sam was definitely my favorite relation. "Still a lot of boxes left to unpack?"

"I could make a fort out of them," I replied with a laugh.

"And you probably should," she said, her tone sobering slightly. "Don't want you to get in a tangle with those city wolves."

I didn't answer.

Her voice softened. "There's trouble, isn't there."

I nodded even though she couldn't see me. "Lots of trouble, Aunt Sam. I've got to get Mom outta here before it gets worse."

"Is it going to get worse?"

"It could, a lot worse. I'm worried she's going to get caught in the middle of it."

I could almost hear her planning. "Well, you're caught in the middle of it then, too. Can't you come with Vicki?"

Part of me ached to be away from all of this, to leave the werewolf mess behind and never look back. But now that I knew what Mason was up to, I couldn't walk away, not if I could stop him before he hurt someone else. "I can't. I need to be here to clear up some things."

She fell silent for a minute, than spoke quietly, her voice full of concern. "It sounds dangerous."

I never pulled any punches with Aunt Sam. "It is. But I can handle it."

Silence fell again and I gave her the time she needed. Aunt Sam was a compulsive planner. I knew if I could get her on my side, things would be a lot easier. She finally spoke. "Okay, I'm telling Vicki that Brody's sick and I need her help with the kids. Think she'll go for that?"

"I do." Uncle Brody had immune system problems and when he was sick he couldn't do anything. Mom would feel obligated to help out like she had done many times before. "That would be perfect. Thank you so much."

"No problem. And Jaze?"

I paused. "Yeah?"

Her voice warmed. "Take care of yourself. You shouldn't have to deal with all of this on your own and I worry about you."

I worry about me, too, I thought, but didn't say it out loud. "Thanks, Aunt Sam. I really appreciate your help."

"Love you," she replied.

"Love you, too, bye."

When I hung up the phone, I felt relieved and more stressed at the same time. Knowing Aunt Sam, she would have plane tickets purchased and Mom on her way within the next day or two. I dreaded being alone. Already, the darkness of the house closed in like a coffin. I pushed back my chair and stepped outside. The humid night air didn't help much, reminding me that I was in an unfamiliar city fighting what could easily be a losing battle. I turned to go back inside when

I heard the neighbor's door slide open.

The breeze told of Nikki and my heart slowed. I cursed myself for what I had said to her. She reached out to me, and out of fear of her parents I had shot her down. I listened to her cross the lawn and sit at the foot of one of their maple trees. I opened our door and closed it as if I had just come out, then crossed the yard and sat with my back against the fence a few feet from her. Just being near her made my heart beat faster, and I had to force my mind to think clearly.

I took a deep breath and let it out in a dramatic sigh, then hit my head back against the fence. "Just stupid," I said softly but loud enough for her to hear.

The grass moved slightly as she shifted her weight.

I sighed again and put my head in my hands. After a moment, I faked an Oscar-worthy sob.

"Jaze, are you okay?" she asked, unable to stay silent any longer.

I shook my head. "It's just horrible. I can't believe it."

Her voice filled with concern and I heard her move closer to the fence. "What? Can I help?"

I turned with a smile she couldn't see in the dark. "I don't know. Can you help me make up with this girl who I totally shot down and was rude to, and who didn't deserve it at all?"

She threw a handful of grass through the slot in the fence. "Oh, Jaze. Grow up," she said with a laugh.

"I really do feel horrible," I told her honestly. "You reached out to me and I acted like an idiot."

"I shouldn't have told you those things," she said, her voice quieter.

I shook my head. "You needed to talk to someone, and why not me. It's not like I've got anywhere to go."

She stuck her hand through the slot in the fence and tried to slap me. I laughed and grabbed it, then on impulse turned her hand over and kissed it softly on the back. "I really am sorry," I whispered; my lips brushed her soft skin. My heart raced at her touch and I grew still, forcing myself to stay focused.

She stopped fighting to pull her hand back and I listened to her breathe softly on the other side of the fence. The moment lengthened with unspoken questions, dangerous questions. I finally let go of her hand and sat back on my heels.

"So, werewolf Hunters, huh?" I asked as nonchalantly as I could.

She pulled her hand back and I could hear the smile in her voice. "Yeah, you must think I'm crazy."

I shook my head, thinking quickly. "No, not really. I mean, when I came to this city I could tell something was strange."

"Really?" The fence creaked as she turned around and sat with her back to it. "How so?"

"Well, the school for one." I forced a laugh. "I've never seen so many metal detectors. And security guards? Isn't that a little overboard?"

She laughed, soft and sweet. "Yeah, I guess people know something's wrong."

I nodded but kept silent. After a minute I turned so that our backs were to each other on opposite sides of the fence.

I swallowed past the dread that filled my chest since she told me her parents killed werewolves; I had to know if they were the Hunters who killed my dad. "So. . . have your parents killed many werewolves?"

Her shoulders slid against the wood in a shrug. "I don't know. I guess so. We go wherever they hear rumors."

"Where have you been?"

"New York and New Jersey, mostly, then Florida and the Dakotas. We spent some time along the Oregon coast, but they didn't find anything." She sighed. "It's all they talk about now. I've finally stopped listening."

I sighed inwardly, muscles easing that I didn't realize had been tense. "You're not into hunting?"

She shook her head and the perfume of her hair wafted over to me. I closed my eyes. "No, not really. I couldn't kill anything, even if it was a blood-thirsty werewolf."

I closed my eyes tighter and rubbed them. "You don't feel the need to avenge your brother?"

She let out her breath slowly and I heard her lean her head back against the fence with an almost inaudible sigh. "That's the question, isn't it? Some demon creature kills your brother, your parents are all gung-ho about wiping them from the face of the earth, and you're left wondering what happened to living life." She reached up a hand and I wondered if she wiped away tears. "The thing is," she said with a sniff, "I think Randy would be sad about the way they've handled all of this."

I sat up slowly and turned around to face the fence. "What do you mean?"

Strands of her black hair had drifted between the planks and stood out in contrast to the lighter wood. She shook her head and they waved in the light night breeze like seaweed caught in an ocean current. "I don't know. It's just. . . ." She fell silent, and then rushed on as though she had been holding the words back for a long time. "Randy wouldn't have wanted them to throw their lives away like this. He always lived each day to its fullest, always went on adventures, on his quests." Her voice fell. "That's how he found the werewolves, his search for 'alternate forms of life'."

"Sounds like quite the guy," I said sincerely.

She nodded and sat up. "He really was."

I frowned, curious now. "How long ago was he killed?"

"Ten years ago; he was fifteen."

My heart stilled. "You mean you've been chasing werewolves after your parents since you were seven?"

"Like I said, crazy, huh?"

I hesitated, then nodded. "Definitely crazy."

She laughed and stood up. "Well, I'd better go in and study. Mrs. Beetle's test is tomorrow, you know."

I rose as well. "Yeah, looking forward to it."

I could make out her smile in the darkness. "Liar."

"Yeah."

She laughed again and made her way to the house. She paused at the door. "Jaze?"

"What?"

She hesitated, then said, "Thanks for listening, and for not laughing."

I shrugged. "It's the least I could do after how I treated you yesterday."

She nodded. "Yes, it is. But you didn't just listen." When I waited, she continued, "You really listened. You cared, and that means a lot to me."

She turned and went into the house, sliding the door quietly shut behind her. "I really do care," I whispered. I shook my head, took one last deep breath of the humid night air, and went back inside.

Chapter 11

The next three days passed surprisingly quietly. My uneasiness grew as the pack continued to ignore me, and I wondered what it meant. Brock and I planned on our walks to and from school, and Nikki and I met in the alley and went to the swap meet grounds at night with what seemed like most of the student body. We didn't run into Mr. Sathing, the security guard, and I wondered what had happened to him.

Mom didn't bring up going to Aunt Samantha's house until Monday night.

"You have to go, Mom. They need you or Aunt Sam wouldn't have asked," I pushed mercilessly.

"I don't want to leave you here alone. This is a new state, a new city, and you've not even been at that school a week yet."

"But Aunt Sam needs you. Besides, things here are fine."

Mom's resolve faltered slightly, then she shook her head. "I worry, Jaze. Maybe you should come with me."

"We both know I can't afford to skip school. I'll be lucky to pass the eleventh grade as it is. Don't worry," I reassured her. "There hasn't been any pack trouble, I'm doing fine in my classes, and I've made some friends. It's not like I'll be alone." I forced my face to remain expressionless on the last part.

Mom sighed and her tone softened. She looked at me across the fried chicken and mashed potatoes she had picked up on her way home. "I don't want to leave until after Wednesday."

"Why Wednesday?" I asked, though we both knew. My bones ached, longing to phase and run.

"I don't want you to be alone for your first phase in a new city."

I didn't point out that I had already phased in order to save Brock. Reminding her that there were hostile werewolves in the area would only make matters worse. "It'll be okay, Mom. I have a plan."

"You do?" she asked skeptically.

I nodded. "I'm going to lock myself in the basement. That way when I phase I can't get out anyway. There's no way I can get into trouble."

She looked me over carefully, then finally said, "Sam bought me a ticket for tomorrow before she even spoke to me. I don't know why she does that."

"She must really need you," I replied; I inwardly thanked Aunt Sam for her foresight.

Mom sighed. "I guess so. I can't really turn her down now, can I?"

I shook my head. "Don't worry, Mom. I'll be fine. You can call me whenever you want."

She rose from the table and started packing away the remaining pieces of uneaten chicken. I scooped the mashed potatoes back into their Styrofoam container and poured the gravy on top.

"I'll leave you some money for food, and you'll have the car. If there's an emergency or you get bored you can go to Brock's," she said, her eyebrows pulled together in worry.

I smiled at her. "I'll be fine."

She shook her head. "It's just bad timing. And after what happened to your father, I don't like to leave you alone." She fidgeted with the chicken bucket.

I grabbed her hand and held it until she looked at me. "Mom, I'll be okay," I said, softer now. "You need a break, too, you know."

She gave me a small smile. "Maybe you're right. It's been so hard with the new job and everything. I'm lucky they'll let me work long distance for a week or so. My boss' brother has the same condition Brody does, so he's sympathetic." Her voice wavered, "A break would be nice."

"Go, Mom. You deserve it. And you'd have a good time with Sam and the kids."

She nodded in agreement and smiled at me. "You're a good son, you know?"

I grinned. "I know."

We finished cleaning up the table in amiable silence. A tremendous sense of relief washed over me at the thought that at least Mom would be somewhere safe if Mason tried anything.

'Let him,' I muttered under my breath. Mom glanced at me and I threw her another grin.

***

"Be right back," Mom yelled.

I heard the front door shut and ran down the stairs. We needed to take off for the airport in about five minutes. I yanked open the front door. "Where are you going?" She stopped halfway across our lawn. "Just asking the neighbors to keep an eye on you, that's all."

"Wait, Mom!" I protested. She paused, but I couldn't come up with a way to tell her that I didn't want the Hunters next door to know that her werewolf son would be all alone for the next week or so. I shrugged, exasperated. "Never mind."

She shook her head and continued to the neighbor's front door. I hurried back to our porch out of sight and listened. A woman, definitely not Nikki, answered the door.

"Hi," my mom said in her charming way that warmed everyone's hearts. "We just moved in next door and I haven't had the chance to introduce myself yet."

"Oh, yes. I've been meaning to bring you a welcome basket; I'm just not that great a cook. I didn't want you to up and move out again," Nikki's mom replied with a self-deprecating laugh. My blood thickened at the sound of her voice. I waited for her to say something Hunterish. Realizing how stupid that was, I sighed and leaned against our door.

"Well, I'm Vicki Carso and it's a pleasure to meet you," Mom said kindly.

"Meg Valen, the pleasure is mine. I'm glad that you took the initiative and came over!" Nikki's mom sounded friendly, but I knew it was just a ruse.

"Why, thank you," Mom replied. Silence fell for a second and she stumbled over her words. "I, uh, oh, I almost forgot why I came over!" She and Mrs. Valen laughed like longtime friends. "I'm leaving on a trip and my son, Jaze, will be alone.

I was just hoping you could help keep an eye on things."

"Oh, most definitely. Nikki mentioned that a nice boy lived next door." I snorted a quiet laugh. "Is everything alright? I mean, is it a family emergency?"

"My brother-in-law is sick, so I'm going to help my sister with her kids. It's not really an emergency, it's just-"

"She needs you there," Mrs. Valen concluded.

"Exactly," Mom agreed. She sighed. "I just hate to leave Jaze and I worry so much, but he's behind already what with the move and everything."

"Don't worry about a thing. We'll take good care of him," Mrs. Valen replied in a sweet voice. I bared my teeth.

"Thank you so much," Mom said. "I really, really appreciate it. And I hope we can get to know each other better when I get back."

"Me, too," Nikki's mother said with what I assume she thought was sincerity. "I'm glad you moved next door. We'll have to get together!"

Mom bade her goodbye and came back across the lawn. I shook my head when she came into view and held the door open for her. "There," she said with a smug smile. "I survived our first meeting with the neighbor. What did you think they'd do, bite me?"

They would do much more than that if they knew our secret, but I let it go. "You're right, Mom. I don't know why I worry so much. Just careful, I guess."

The laugh lines around her eyes deepened and she pulled me close in a hug. "You have too much to worry about for someone your age. Stop trying to protect me and start living your life."

"Yes, Mom," I mumbled.

She laughed and mussed my hair.

I dropped Mom off at the airport the next evening and had to fight back the feeling that it could be the last time I would see her if things went wrong. She hesitated and paced by the car, stalling. "I don't know," she protested. "I shouldn't be leaving you."

I smiled reassuringly. "Go, Mom. Aunt Sam will be devastated if you don't arrive on that plane."

We both knew it was true and she gave me one last hug. "Take care of yourself." She said it as a command. "I love you."

"I love you, too," I told her. I gave her an extra long hug, which seemed to surprise her because her arms tightened around me and she sighed.

"We're going to be okay," she said quietly.

"Yes, we are," I agreed; I hoped with all my heart that it was true.

She took a deep breath and stepped away, luggage in one hand and her ticket in the other. She gave one last longing look toward the car.

"Go, Mom," I said with a laugh.

She shook her head, smiled, and walked through the sliding doors. I watched after her for a moment, then got in our beat up car and headed home.

***

The lights were dark when I pulled up to our tiny house. I went straight to the backyard. I punched the bag and smiled grimly at the familiar bite of cloth on my ungloved knuckles. The moon's rays drifted conspicuously through the trees as if to remind me that tomorrow I would have to submit to its will. I punched two quick low jabs followed by an uppercut, then stepped back and kicked it high. The bag rattled on its chain.

"Have some pent up frustration?" a voice asked from the next yard.

I turned, dismayed I had let my guard down enough to not even check if anyone was around. If it had been a werewolf or a Hunter, I could be dead. I stepped closer to the fence. "Just feeling a little antsy, that's all."

"Something a good game of hockey could fix?" Nikki asked.

Her skates hit together with an inviting clack, but I shook my head. "I'm not really feeling it tonight."

Nikki stepped on the board across the bottom of the fence and levered herself up so that she could look into our yard. She smiled when she saw me, though it was too dark for her to make out my features. "What's wrong, Jaze? You're never down."

I smiled bitterly at that. "As far as you know."

She paused for a moment, then levered herself to the top board of the fence. I hurried over and helped her down on my side. She studied me for a moment, her hands on her hips. "You seem different."

"Oh, really," I replied, wondering why I couldn't shake the harshness of my tone. "And you know me so well?" She pursed her lips in a small smile as though she was trying not to laugh. "I think I do, tough boy. And I think you need to talk."

I shook my head. "I'm not the talking type." She grabbed my hand and led me to our back porch. "Well, I am, so you're gonna have to loosen up sometime."

She sat on the cement step and pulled me down beside her. We sat in silence and the city sounds surrounded us. Cars honked and a siren sounded in the distance. Crickets and cicadas each fought to sing louder than the other. A slight breeze moved the leaves above us and tickled through the grass. Far away, a lone wolf howled at the night. I felt the call of the change, the call that would be impossible to ignore tomorrow. My muscles tightened.

Nikki was still holding my arm and glanced at me. "What is it?"

I shook my head. "Nothing." I stood up, making her let go. "I'm sorry, Nikki. I'm not very good company tonight."

She rose with me and tipped her head toward the back door. "I understand if you don't want to talk, but being the good friend that I am, I can't let you wallow away with your frustrations all alone. Let's watch a movie or something."

My heart stuttered and I glanced at her house. "Your parents won't care?"

She shrugged and a hurt expression swept across her eyes. "They won't notice I'm gone." Then she smiled past it. "And anyways, I've never seen inside your house."

I laughed despite my foul mood. "It's the same as yours. The real estate agent said all the houses on the block were made with the same floor plan."

She shook her head teasingly. "I'll bet you don't have the same color scheme." She slid the door open and stepped inside, leaving me standing on my own stoop.

I stared after her for a moment, then shook my head and followed her in.

"So this is what the house of the impenetrable Jaze Carso looks like, huh?" she asked when I found her sorting through movies in the living room.

I watched her in silence, unsure what to say.

She ran her fingers down the stack I had left by the television since I hadn't unpacked the stand yet. "Hmm, pretty good taste here. You cover most topics, though a bit slim on the chick flicks." Her finger stopped and she threw me a look. "Bed of Roses?"

"That's my mom's," I protested. A faint blush touched my cheeks at her scrutiny.

"Okay, I'll give you that one." She got to the bottom of the stack. "You have all the Rambos?"

I grinned. "Only the best movies for my lady."

She laughed and pulled out the set. "Well, then we're in for a movie marathon night. You up for it?"

"You want to watch Rambo?" I asked skeptically.

"'You are not expendable'," she quoted with the beautiful smile that showed her perfect teeth. "How romantic is that?"

I laughed. "Okay, okay. But I've never known a girl who thinks Rambo is romantic."

She nodded as if satisfied and threw herself on the couch. "Well, then you've never met a girl like me."

"You got that right," I agreed wholeheartedly.

She slapped my arm and I took the movie from her and put it in the player. When I sat down, she kicked off her shoes, curled her legs up underneath her, and lifted my arm around her shoulders so that she cuddled against my chest.

My heart pounded at her proximity and I wondered if she could hear it.

When the concluding credits rolled past, I realized I had missed the entire movie by watching her instead. Nikki jumped up and grabbed the case. "Next one?"

I shrugged and fought back a smile. "Why not?"

As she put in the next movie, I wondered how on earth I had gotten so lucky. She curled back under my arm and leaned against my side. "Jaze?"

"Yeah?" I asked.

"Thanks for moving next door."

I smiled. "No problem."

She rested her head against my chest and turned to watch Rambo's next conquest.

Chapter 12

"When you say movie marathon, you mean it," I said into Nikki's hair.

She laughed sleepily and pushed herself up. She had fallen asleep on the couch, her head on my shoulder and me against the corner where one of Mom's books stuck painfully into my back, but I couldn't bear to wake her so had ignored it.

I sat up and gave her a teasing smile. "Rambo didn't hold your attention?"

"After the three-hundredth kill I sort of dozed off," she admitted with a smile.

"That's okay, me too," I lied. I couldn't fall asleep, not with her so close, trusting me with everything even though I didn't feel worthy of that trust.

She stood up and brushed her hair back from her face. It stood up in places from sleeping, but I didn't tell her. It made her all the more adorable and I imagined this is what it would be like waking up with her every morning.

I shook my head to clear it of such impossible thoughts. I would never get married. Dad's death had devastated Mom to the point that she was no longer the same person she had been before. She walked the house like a shadow, as if she saw our old place and then wondered why we were here instead. When she thought I wasn't looking, she stared at the picture of Dad in the hallway, the one where he stood next to a smoking barbecue grill, a lighter in one hand and a bottle of lighter fluid in the other. The smoke billowed so heavily you could barely see him, but the grin on his face was the one I remembered, the one that showed in my mind when I thought of him.

I shied away from wondering who I had become since he was killed. I knew I wasn't the same, and would never be again. Being a werewolf was not glamorous or beautiful. It was a life of danger and death and I would never bring a family into it.

"What are you thinking about?" Nikki asked quietly, studying my face. "You look so sad."

I rubbed a hand over my eyes to clear away the dark thoughts. "Unhappy things," I replied.

When she saw I wasn't going to expound, she gave me a sweet look that made my heart stutter. "You can let me in, Jaze. It helps, trust me."

I shook my head, my walls grudgingly rising back up. "Not with this."

She smiled in understanding. "Okay then, whenever you're ready."

"Thanks," I said, though I knew that I would never be.

"I guess that's my cue to go." She went to the door and I regretted my standoffish mood.

"Nikki, I'm sorry."

She turned, her hand on the doorknob. "It's okay. I know how it is to hold things inside. Sometimes you feel like you can't talk to anyone, like the whole world is against you." My heart rang true with her words. She smiled sadly. "But you have to trust someone, Jaze. You can't carry the weight of the world by yourself. You helped me, and I'll be there to help you if you're ever at that jumping off point." She opened the front door, threw me one last smile, then closed it behind her.

I stared at the door for a long time, fighting a battle I knew I couldn't win. I fell asleep that night with a nightmare of werewolves chasing Nikki down a dark road. She stopped at the end and turned, a silver knife in her hand. A wolf jumped at her and she impaled it. The wolf fell to the ground, lifeless. When I got closer, I realized the wolf was my dad.

***

I walked slowly to school with Brock the next morning. My arms and legs tingled in anticipation of the coming night's phase. It wasn't usually that bad, but Dad and I had never gone so long without phasing. We used to run maybe two or three nights a week through the woods a mile from our house. We would chase deer, run through streams, and race so fast that I felt like we were flying across the ground. My muscles ached for that release, and anticipation shivered through me even though I knew I would be locked in the basement, unable to take part in the monthly run.

"So tonight, huh?" Brock asked, guessing my thoughts.

I nodded.

"Are you worried about the pack?"

"I'll be staying inside," I said, though the regret in my voice was undeniable.

He glanced at me and mercifully changed topics. "You ready for Mr. Henry's math test?"

I shook my head. "Algebra was never my strong subject. And for some reason, I can't keep my mind on studying."

"For some reason," Brock laughed pointedly.

I glanced at him. "What does that mean?"

Brock grinned. "Oh, come on. I hang around enough to notice that you have a budding relationship with a certain neighbor, who also happens to be in a relationship with a certain Alpha werewolf, if you know what I mean."

"It's not like that!" I protested.

He laughed again. "All I know is Nikki Valen never so much as smiled at me until you were around. Now, it's like we're in this secret club." His voice took on an awed quality. "She even winked at me the other day when I walked past her and Chet in the hall. I'm lucky he didn't see or I'd be dead right now!"

I laughed despite my somber mood. "Yeah, well, we're just friends. I'm sure Chet has no idea."

He grinned. "You better hope so. That's one werewolf I never want to face."

I nodded in agreement, though like any werewolf in another's territory, I wondered deep down which of us would win. I shook myself to clear the dangerous thoughts. By the time we entered the school, Brock's good humor lifted my mood enough to help me push down the reminder of what the night would bring.

***

I locked myself inside the unfinished basement long before midnight, knowing the closer I came to phasing, the harder it would be to listen to my brain instead of my soul. I longed to run, but I also wanted to survive the night.

I paced the floor, tracing cracks in the cement. The scent of fresh earth seeped through, moist from the recent rains. I breathed it in deeply and held it, and was reminded of forest runs at midnight, ancient oaks stretching toward the sky, rich loam soft underfoot, the faint trail of a rabbit, and the flick of a white tail as deer left the meadow.

A shudder ran through me and I opened my eyes. Moonlight streamed through the tiny window in the far corner. Though I couldn't see the moon, I could feel its fullness. It called to me and I had no choice but to answer.

I took off my clothes and waited. The need to phase increased until I let go of my control with a shudder. Seconds later, my bones began to change; some lengthened and others shortened, pulling me in familiar directions. My fingers withdrew into paws. I stretched and rolled my shoulders, not fighting it now. Phasing ached, but it was like stretching muscles that hadn't been used in a long time and I relished the slight pains of my scars and the ache of the few remaining bruises on my back from the drunk driver.

My mouth and nose elongated into a muzzle. My teeth rounded and sharpened, and ached to tear into something. My skin itched a second before coarse black fur followed by a softer undercoat grew along my body. I pushed my paws out on the floor as far as they could go, then shook and was a wolf.

Even my werewolf-heightened senses as a human were no match for what I had in wolf form. A breeze escaped through a crack in the corner of the small window above me and

113

tickled tantalizingly along my muzzle, beckoning me to follow it past the city to the rolling hills and forests beyond. I couldn't follow it, and paced madly around the tiny basement. What had seemed a safe haven before was now a prison.

Howls caught my ears, angry and challenging. They came closer until the wolves circled the house, calling me out. Chet had decided to wait until the full moon, until I couldn't avoid the change any longer, in order to challenge me to the duel for leadership instinct demanded of two Alphas in the same territory.

I regarded the angry golden eyes in the window and my lips pulled back in a silent snarl. Wolves dug around the window sill; their claws scraped against the cement foundation. The black wolf stared at me, hatred and domination in his eyes. Chet in wolf form was even more ruled by the wolf instincts to defend his pack against a stranger, especially an Alpha. I hadn't planned for the basement to be a fortress, but the decision was proving more insightful than I had realized.

After about an hour of pacing, the wolves stopped their angry howls. I wondered vaguely if Nikki's parents, the Hunters, had heard them, but no yelping or sounds of pursuit followed their near silent trek from my house. I listened with a crazy, vain longing to go with them despite the danger, to run with a pack again, to perhaps lead the pack myself.

I shook hard to clear the desperate thoughts, then sat by the window and soaked in what I could of the moonlight. It caressed my fur, a gentle touch that brought a comfort and peace I hadn't known since the night Dad was killed. I longed to break through the window so I could bask in it unhindered. I looked closer at the window and realized I could.

114

The promise of an unfettered run through the night was too much to bear. I backed up, my muscles coiled tightly, and was about to spring when another pair of wolf eyes appeared in the window. A snarl of pent up frustration ripped from my lips. The wolf dropped on its belly, its head barely visible in the window now. I caught a faint whine and pricked my ears in surprise. The wolf pawed at the window, not angry or hasty but as if submitting to me. I trotted cautiously to the wall beneath it and sniffed.

Mouse! I gazed at him in surprise. The lone wolf, Brock's quiet friend, had defied the pack's anger and come to my house. I stared at him for a moment, unsure why he would do such a thing. He met my eyes, then dropped his gaze and pulled his ears back. Without warning, he butted his head into the window. A small cracking noise sounded and more fresh air leaked through. I realized what he was doing and growled a quiet warning. He backed up from the window.

I trotted to the back of the basement, then turned and ran. After three short strides I gathered my legs underneath me and jumped. I flattened my ears and ducked my head, hitting the window with the top of my skull. It shattered easily and I pulled through into the fresh night air. I shook the glass from my fur and gazed around. The full moon basked the night in its pale glow; mile upon unexplored mile beckoned to me. I inhaled deeply and let it out through my nose, my brain categorizing the new scents as quickly as they came.

Mouse rolled over on the grass and I glanced at him; I had forgotten his presence in the gift of freedom. He looked at me with his belly exposed, his mousy gray fur soft and fine. I took a few steps toward the street. Mouse rose slowly to his feet and watched me. He whined quietly in his throat. I debated whether it would be safe for him to come with me, but he had already risked so much I couldn't leave him to the mercy of Chet's pack. I gave a sharp bark and he trotted up and wagged his tail. I snorted and took off. Mouse followed close behind.

It felt so good to run, to forget about Mason, my dad, the school, Chet's pack, and Nikki's parents. Everything fell away with the pounding of my paws against the pavement. We ran until streetlights no longer showed the way, then I dove into the underbrush along the side of the road with Mouse at my heels. We darted through the trees, two ghosts scaring up wildlife in the split second before we passed and left them far behind.

We ran the entire night. Mouse and I followed game trails that twisted between rolling greens hills and through cow pastures. We darted through fields of sleeping geese and swam across lazy, winding rivers. Mouse loosened up from the shy, submissive wolf and bounded around me like a puppy with a new bone. We ran through the trees until the moon went down and we stayed in wolf form of our own free will.

We only caught scent of the werewolf pack once the entire night, and we stayed far clear of them until they were gone. It was freedom. Not the freedom I was used to or that my Alpha instincts longed for, but it was far better than staying locked in a basement all night chasing the moon through my dreams.

Mouse and I crept back to my house in the early hours of the morning. He grabbed up a pack of clothes in his jaws he had hidden behind the bushes, and we slipped through the broken basement window and phased.

"I'll have to get that fixed before Mom returns," I said, pulling on my shirt.

Mouse glanced at it. "Yeah, you never know what kind of pests might show up." He threw me a grin, shy and timid now that we were back in human form.

I studied him and he met my gaze for a minute before dropping his eyes. "That was a risky thing you did," I said quietly.

He looked at the floor. "I know. I just. . . ." He glanced back up and his eyes flashed. "I just get so tired of Chet and his pack. Everything has to be done his way, everyone has to follow him and listen to him."

I fought back a smile. "That's kind of the way it is with Alphas."

He shook his head. "Not like that, at least not the way my dad used to do it."

I stared at him. "Your dad was an Alpha."

He nodded. "*The* Alpha, until he died."

I frowned. "But you've got a gray coat."

"My mom's human." He glanced at me curiously. "Like yours, right?"

"Yeah," I admitted, "I shouldn't have been born an Alpha, but I was. I can't explain it."

Mouse shrugged. "Maybe you can take the pack from Chet. It'd be a lot better off."

I held up a hand. "Let's not get hasty. The pack is his and I don't want it. There's something going on here and I need to get to the bottom of it before anyone else gets hurt."

"Anyone else?"

I meet Mouse's eyes, wondering how much I dared to tell him, how much he could take. I took a deep breath. "Someone is killing off all the older wolves and Alphas."

His eyes widened in shock. "Why?" When he realized his own father would have been included in this, his voice dropped. "Who would do such a thing?"

The pain in his voice echoed the ache in my heart and I fought to speak. "They want control of the packs, all of them, as far as I can tell, and eliminating the stronger wolves is the best way to do it."

Mouse's eyes darkened and he glared at me, not realizing the challenge he gave. "Who?"

I shook off the instinct to fight such a challenge. "I have reason to believe it's my father's brother, Mason. I saw him here a few days ago. He not an Alpha, but close, and he definitely has the ambition for power. I wouldn't put it past him."

Mouse stared at me for a couple of seconds, then seemed to realize what he was doing and dropped his eyes. "Your father was killed, too?"

I nodded.

"By his own brother?" his voice was incredulous and tinged with bitterness.

I nodded again and turned away with the pretense of picking up glass. He joined me.

"That's messed up," he said quietly after a while.

"I know," I replied in as calm a voice as I could manage.

He sat down against the wall and toyed with the shards of glass he held. I watched him, concerned about what he might do. He twirled one short shard between his thumb and forefinger. "And you're planning to kill him?" he asked, though it was more of a statement than a question.

I shrugged, but my voice was determined. "Whatever it takes."

He nodded. "Then count me in."

I stared at him. "You don't want to get tangled up in this."

He glanced up at me, a small, bitter smile on his face. "I don't know if you noticed, but your uncle counted me in a long time ago."

I studied him for a minute; the determination in his eyes gave no room for argument. I nodded despite the pit in my stomach. I didn't want anyone else to get hurt, but if he felt he had to fight, I couldn't blame him because I had the same reasons he did. "Okay. Glad to have you with me."

He gave me another small smile. "We make quite the pack, don't we?"

I laughed, but the comment eased something in my chest. "Yeah, we do. Let's go get something to eat."

He followed me up the wooden stairs and I unlocked the padlock I had used.

Mouse glanced at me and I grinned sheepishly. "To keep me from escaping as a wolf," I explained. We both looked back at the broken window and laughed.

Chapter 13

When Brock and I walked to school the next morning, I felt better than I had in a long time. Running through the woods in wolf form turned out to be better therapy than I could have imagined. I still kicked myself for breaking free, wondering what would have happened if the pack had caught up to us, but I didn't regret feeling as though a load had been lifted off my shoulders, if only for a short time.

"Enjoy your, uh, werewolf time?" Brock asked with a puzzled smile.

"Yeah, actually," I admitted. I decided not to tell him about Mouse. Mouse must have had his own reasons to keep it from his friend if he had made it this far without Brock finding out.

"You definitely seem like you're in a better mood."

I laughed. "I'm that bad, huh?"

He grinned and ran a hand through his spiky brown hair without saying anything.

"No answer, huh? That must be pretty bad." I glanced at him out of the corner of my eye. "Why do you hang out with me?"

This time, he was the one to laugh. "Actually, considering the fact that you are a werewolf, you're pretty mild tempered." At my questioning look, he rushed on, "From what I've read, werewolves are moody even in their human form. Something about the instincts and territorial aggression, I don't know." Then he looked at me and his voice became serious. "You saved my life, Jaze. You didn't even know me. You could have let them tear me apart."

I tried to push down the mild hurt I felt and had to acknowledge the werewolf moodiness. "So that's the reason you're still around; you feel you owe me something for saving you?" I joked half-heartedly.

He shrugged, then shook his head. "Well, no. You're different than anyone I know. You're. . ." he searched for the word, hesitated, then said it quickly. "Loyal."

I snorted, but realized the truth. In the transition between losing my father, moving to a new territory filled with hostile werewolves, and trying to find my own place in the world, Brock had become part of my own tiny pack I had created to hold my sanity together. I glanced at him, wondering if he suspected it, and realized he probably did. I frowned and tried to form words out of my thoughts, but he held up a hand.

"I'm honored, you know? It's weird, all of this, but I'm glad to be here." He slapped me on the shoulder and laughed. "Besides, it's gotten me closer to Nikki, which has also gotten me closer to her hot girlfriends."

I laughed and punched him lightly in the shoulder. "Always after the girls, aren't you?"

He shrugged. "What else is there?"

***

We went to Brock's after school; the thought of staying in the empty house alone kept me away as long as possible.

School had gone well. I found out I actually passed my math test, only by one question, but at least I passed. It rained during lunch, then the sun came out to dry everything so that the world smelled fresh and new. Chet and his pack had also been absent, which added to the greatness of the day. I supposed I should have been worried about where they were, but figured he had already ruined enough days that I got to keep one for myself once in a while.

We watched television, ate some pizza compliments of Brock's mom, and were lounging on the porch drinking sodas when the rhythmic pounding of running feet caught my ears. A figure dashed up the road toward us through the twilight. Brock noticed my attention was elsewhere and followed my eyes.

"Who is it?" he asked, squinting to see through the shadows.

The figure was upwind and when his scent came to me I set down the soda and stood. Fear and sweat mingled with Mouse's woody, homey scent of Italian food and a wood burning stove. Somewhere in the back of my mind I pictured a tiny, rotund, Italian speaking grandmother wrapped in a shawl and apron and holding a bowl of sauce. I shook my head to clear the image. "Mouse."

"Jaze?" Mouse shouted.

I ran to meet him, Brock at my heels. Mouse nearly bowled into me, then bent over with his hands on his knees gasping for air. "You've got to go," he forced out.

"Go where?" I demanded; adrenaline rose at the panic in his voice.

Mouse glanced up at me, his eyes wide with fear. "The pack, they're after Nikki."

My heart slowed. I put my hands on his shoulders. "What are you talking about? Nikki is Chet's girlfriend."

Mouse shook his head, his chest heaving. "Something about Nikki's parents. One of the werewolves was hurt last night, and they think her parents had something to do with it. The pack waited all day for them to show up, but they never did, so they're going to attack Nikki in revenge."

I had my shirt off before he finished speaking.

Brock grabbed my arm. "Jaze, what are you doing?"

I pulled free and stepped away. "I've got to save her, Brock. They'll kill her."

"Why?" he asked.

"Her parents are Hunters."

Brock's mouth fell open, but he made no attempt to stop me.

I phased to wolf form faster than I ever had before. The world spun dizzily around me, but I ducked my head and ran down the sidewalk. I pushed into the wolf's mile-eating lope until I practically flew. My paws barely touched the ground. I rounded the corner and ran up the street.

Images of Nikki being torn apart by the pack flew through my head. I saw her body lying in pieces on her front lawn the way my dad's had in our living room. I pushed myself faster, and turned the corner of her block in time to see Nikki surrounded on the sidewalk in front of her house.

Five of Chet's pack were still in human form, including Chet himself. Silver blades flashed in the streetlight. The other six had already phased to wolf form. Their teeth were bared in snarling white flashes against the darkening night. I was shocked by their audacity at appearing in wolf form in the middle of the city. Chet leaned toward Nikki, his face inches from hers. He held a knife and gestured as though threatening to use it.

I ran toward them at full speed. No one saw or heard me until I was less than a second away, and by then it was too late. I plowed headlong through the surrounding pack. My shoulders impacted two wolves and they yelped and flew to the sides. I barreled into Chet, knocking him to the ground, then spun so that Nikki was at my back and the rest of them were at the front. A low growl rumbled in my chest.

Chet rose shakily to his feet, his gaze wide as his looked around for his attacker. When his eyes fell on me, they filled with such bitter hatred I fought to keep from tearing him apart right there. "Nice of you to join us, Jaze," he spat out. Blood trickled down his lip and he wiped it away with the back of his hand. He stepped forward, his knife low. "I'm going to enjoy this."

I backed up slowly, forcing Nikki to step back until she stood against the fence. I glanced back and her eyes met mine, wide and searching. Chet stepped closer. I turned back to him and growled. He didn't need to be in wolf form to understand the threat of my tone.

Chet laughed, a dark chuckle that made my fur stand on end. "If that's the way you want it." He stepped back to phase and motioned for his pack to attack.

Five wolves and five werewolves in human form dove at me. I ducked under a wolf from the left and he collided with one on the right. I jumped on their tangle of bodies and launched myself at two of the werewolves in human form. I caught one knife-baring hand in my jaws as the force of my body barreled them to the ground. I rolled to the right, pulling the one I held over my back and to the ground on the other side. He yelled when his arm snapped and he dropped the knife.

I dodged a knife swipe from another human, spun to the left, and grappled head on with a wolf. He snapped at my stomach, but I barreled him over with my shoulder and held him to the ground. I clamped onto his throat and bit down. Warm blood filled my mouth. The instinct to close my teeth and finish him took over. He squirmed as I tightened my jaw. A blow to the side threw me over, breaking my hold. I rose and dodged to the right in time to avoid another wolf. Then Nikki screamed.

Chet, hulking and huge in his Alpha form, closed the distance between them. His black fur blended in with the rapidly gathering night, but his eyes glowed golden and angry in the darkness. I leaped over the two wolves between us and was about to reach him when something slammed into my ribs. Pain laced out in all directions, fogging my vision with red. I gasped for breath as I turned to face my attacker.

Darryl, one of the wolves I had fought to protect Brock, stood still in his human form, a silver knife in one hand. He waved it at me and drops of my blood fell to the lawn. I leaped at him, but was bowled over by two wolves from the left. I rolled back to my feet fast enough to throw one of the wolves and bite out at the other one when Darryl sliced again with the knife. This time, it buried to the hilt in my stomach. I grabbed his shoulder in my teeth before he could step back and pulled him to the ground.

He yelled and rolled over; his feet caught me in the ribs and he kicked me away. I landed on my back. Blood streamed from my wounds, taking my strength with it. I forced myself up by sheer will. Wolves surrounded me. Nikki screamed again and I glanced up in time to see Chet jump at her. I launched myself over the heads of the wolves and landed on Chet's back. He rolled over just short of Nikki, teeth flashing. His jaws snapped shut millimeters from my jugular. I dodged out of the way, then lunged at his shoulder and tore a gash down his forearm.

A blaze of pain ran down my back. I spun to see another werewolf in human form backing away as fast as he could. I dove at him and a rumbling howl escaped my throat. He tripped over a wolf and fell. I lunged for his throat and he held up an arm. I ground it between my teeth and felt the bones snap before he dropped the knife.

Teeth tore at my shoulder. I turned to meet Chet's brutal attack. He dove for my throat, but I met him tooth for tooth. I tried to reach his eyes to blind him, but he was relentless and strong. The silver that coursed through my veins from the knives began to weaken my muscles along with the blood loss from the gaping wounds. His teeth found purchase in my forearm and he bit down. I reached the side of his throat and threw him with a jerk of my neck. He rolled on the lawn and leaped back, ready to attack again, when a gunshot shook the air.

I glanced back to see Nikki standing in the gate holding a shotgun above her head. "This is loaded with silver bullets," she threatened, bringing it down to aim at Chet. "Get away from him."

Chet backed up slowly, his ears held tight to his skull and teeth bared. I faced him until he joined the rest of his pack. Only two were still in human form, and they leaned on each other, bloody and bruised. The rest of the wolves gathered around Chet, awaiting his orders. He growled again and took a step in my direction, but Nikki left the fence and made her way to me, the gun pointed at him like she knew how to use it.

Chet growled his frustration, then turned and stalked down the road, his pack close behind.

Pain knifed through every vein as the silver from the splintered knives spread through my body. I collapsed just as Nikki reached me. Too weak to hold wolf form any longer, I phased on the lawn. My wounds stretched and tore. I couldn't hold back the yell that escaped my lips. I glanced up at Nikki. She held the shotgun with the barrel pointed toward the grass. The silver burned and my whole body felt like it was on fire. It was all I could do to keep from screaming. I could barely think past the pain. My vision blurred red and a shudder coursed through my body. I couldn't stand it anymore. I couldn't live, not like this. I opened my mouth to ask Nikki to shoot me and end it all when I heard a yell.

"Don't touch him!" Brock shouted. His pounding feet raced toward us. He threw his body over mine. "Don't you dare hurt him," he growled in a voice that would have done a werewolf proud.

I glanced up one last time. Nikki's blue eyes met mine and tears spilled down her cheeks. I closed my eyes and let the pain carry me away.

Chapter 14

Voices spoke beyond a door, muffled by the daze of pain.

"Step away from the door, Nikki."

"No!" My senses quickened at the fear in her voice. "He saved my life, Mom!"

"It doesn't matter. He's a werewolf."

"It does too matter! I would have been killed. Chet's an Alpha!"

"Really?" her mom replied. I heard the forced surprise in her voice and realized that she had already known.

Nikki must have heard it, too. "You knew all this time?" Her voice rose, hurt and angry. "You set me up?"

"It wasn't like that, darling," a male voice that must have belonged to Nikki's father said in a placating tone.

The door gave a thump as Nikki leaned against it. "You knew I was dating a werewolf and you didn't tell me? What am I to you, just some bait you can dangle to catch the black coats?"

"We had to know, Nikki," her mother said with a touch of embarrassment.

Nikki fell silent, then spoke again, her voice reluctant as though she didn't want to hear. "Know what?"

Footsteps drew closer to the door. "There's something going on. There has to be older Alphas, but Chet was the only one we could find. We hoped he would lead us to them."

"And by us you meant me?"

A sigh, then, "Yes. You were the only one who had a chance to get close to him."

"He almost killed me for it!" Nikki's voice rose again. "You didn't think to warn me? You know, 'Carry some silver bullets, darling, just in case your boyfriend goes psycho?'"

"We didn't think it would get this far," her father put in. "We thought we'd find the other Alphas long before now."

"Yeah, well, he would have killed me. His whole pack came to tear me apart." I heard Nikki's hand touch the door. "I'd be dead right now if it wasn't for Jaze."

"Another werewolf," her mother said with contempt in her voice.

"Another Alpha," Nikki corrected her softly.

Silence followed.

The door creaked in protest as Nikki leaned more firmly against it. Her elbow brushed the doorknob.

"Why is he still in there?" her mom asked, quieter now. "If he's an Alpha, he should have healed already."

I heard the slide of Nikki's hair across the wood as she shook her head. "They used silver blades, and parts of them broke off. I can't get it all cleaned out." Her calm facade broke and her voice cracked. "He's bleeding to death before he can heal."

There was a moment of silence and I could feel the depth of it through my fevered haze. It felt as if the entire world waited for someone to make a decision. Her mom finally cleared her throat. "Well, what are we standing around for? Heaven knows your father and I have extracted silver fragments before."

Their footsteps came to the door. "How do I know you're not going to kill him?" Nikki protested without moving.

Her father spoke gently. "You're going to have to trust us. We owe you one. We promise to take care of him."

My heart tightened at the potential implications and I hoped Nikki would stay in front of the door. I would rather bleed to death than face Hunters like the ones who had killed Dad.

But Nikki stepped back and the door opened slowly. "You owe me more than one," she whispered.

Their footsteps drew near the bed and I closed my eyes. I focused on breathing steadily to calm my thundering heartbeat.

Nikki's mother gave a quick intake of breath. "Other werewolves did this to him?" she asked quietly. "Why would they do such a thing?"

"He stood in their way to protect me," Nikki replied, her tone bitter.

A hand touched my sweat-soaked forehead. "He's got a high fever, probably from the silver. It kicks in fast." She turned away. "We've got to hurry, Roger, or we'll lose him."

Fingers touched my palm and my hand flinched before I could control it. Nikki touched my shoulder reassuringly. "It's okay, they'll help you," she whispered.

I opened my eyes and fought to focus them on her face. "You're not safe here," I whispered. The words burned through my aching throat. I took a shallow breath against the sharp pain in my side.

"They'll keep me safe. Both of us safe," she replied. Her eyes shone through tears. "You just hang in there, okay? Don't you leave me."

Pain from the gash across my stomach made me gasp. I shut my eyes and clenched my teeth in an effort to stay silent.

"Jaze?" she asked, her voice tight with worry.

"It hurts," I forced out.

"Stay with me," she commanded, her voice rising.

I tried to nod, but flashes of light sparked behind my closed eyelids.

"Jaze?" She turned away and shouted, "Mom, Dad, hurry!"

A hum rose, shutting out all other sound. I opened my leaden eyes and saw her face floating above me, her lips tight and tears tracing trails down her cheeks. Black spots danced in my vision. She mouthed my name. I tried to reply, but my limbs felt heavy and weak. I shut my eyes and gave in to the darkness.

***

Fever dreams brought back memories with stark clarity of Mom, Dad, and I together. I saw them from somewhere behind my shoulder, as if I was the observer of this happy family, a stranger drawn by the hauntingly familiar. Dad carried me as a toddler on his shoulders, my dark blond hair long and wild the way he liked it, a tangled mess like a lion's mane, as my mom would say. Dad tossed me up into the air, and I lost sight of my young self in the light of the sun.

The next dream showed the first time I phased. I saw the proud look on Dad's face when he realized I would be an Alpha like him despite the fact that Mom didn't have any werewolf blood. We tore around the kitchen and living room, me with big gangly puppy paws and silky, shaggy fur that would eventually turn into the coarse outer coat and soft inner coat I had now. We crashed around a corner, breaking Mom's blue vase, but she only smiled and shook her head like a proud mother hen.

The dreams flashed forward to my introduction to the pack. Usually pack members waited until the next full moon to bring any children that had phased, but Dad couldn't wait. He called his pack together and they truly seemed happy that one of his offspring would eventually inherit. I glimpsed Uncle Mason near a tree, his dark gray coat blending in with the forest's shadows. He didn't look angry or pleased, just calculating. I wondered if he had already begun his takeover of the North American werewolves.

I fought to break free of the next dream before the memory even solidified. It was too real, the house, the stars, the smell of wood smoke from cozy home fires. The front door glared brilliant red in the night, though it had been softer and more of a Tuscan color in real life. Mom reached the door first and touched it. It opened slowly and the iron scent of blood filled my nose. I ran through the door, ready to protect her, then froze in horror at the scene before me.

I knew who had been killed even before I saw the body. Dad had fought, and fought hard. The scent of his sweat and determination permeated everything. I could also smell the Hunters, at least four of them, and the scent of Uncle Mason, faint as if he had stayed at the door.

I fell to my knees, tears streaming down my face. Mom fainted behind me, her body crumpling gracefully to the floor like a tired dancer. I rose, picked her up, and carried her to the lawn near the sidewalk. The leftovers of the dinner Mom and I had eaten together sat forgotten in their Styrofoam box where Mom had dropped it when she fell. I walked past it into the living room. A pink heart card from Valentine's Day the day before lay among the shattered remains of the lamp and a picture of our family on the floor. I picked up the card in a daze and opened it as if searching for the familiar in a world that had turned upside down. Mom had written on one side and me on the other.

Dear Jason,

I could never have imagined where life would take us when I said yes to you so many Valentine's Days ago. You had your little pink box, afraid to bring it out when we were around your friends because it wasn't manly. Ha ha. But if I could have seen the life we would lead together, I'd again have said yes, yes, yes, a million times yes, because you have made me happier than I ever thought a person could be. Thank you, my dear sweetheart. I look forward to a hundred more Valentine's Days together.

Love,
Vicki

Dad,

Thanks for everything, for loving Mom and me, for working so hard for us, for being there all the time. You're the best Dad ever.

Love,

Jaze

I stared at the card for another minute, then tore it up and made a small pile in the middle of the floor with the shredded paper. I broke the wooden picture frame into splinters and added it, then used a table leg to tear off a part of the banister and added the chunks to the pile. I did it all in a numb daze, avoiding any thought of what was truly going on. I only knew what I had to do to protect Mom and me, to protect Dad.

Last, I carefully gathered the parts of Dad's dismembered body and laid them gently beside the pile. His blood streaked my shirt and hands. His torso had been thrown in the fireplace. I wiped off what I could of the dark ashes, then added it to the pile. It didn't look like him anymore; I could almost imagine that it was a mannequin, a bleeding, too-real mannequin. His head was nowhere to be found, but Hunters usually took the heads because they wrongly believed that a werewolf could bring itself back together and live if it had the head. I found Dad's arms and legs. When the pile was complete, I sat down and stared at it. I sat that way for several minutes, my thoughts too jumbled and dazed with shock to make any sense.

When I realized what I was doing, I forced myself to my feet, stumbled to the garage, and brought back the gas can we used for the lawn mower. I dumped it on the pile of kindling, on Dad's body, and around the living room. The smell of blood and gasoline tangled harshly in the air and I ran outside and threw up in the bushes. I then grabbed a cigarette lighter from the cupboard by the fridge where Mom kept the birthday candles, lit it, and tossed it on the pile. The roar of flames leaping to life followed me out the door.

I watched the house burn long enough to ensure that the flames had a good hold and wouldn't die before our home was a pile of ash, then carried Mom to the car and laid her across the back seat. I looked back once as I drove away. The flaming house burned with the glow of a sunset in my rear view mirror. A fire engine raced past and I turned my attention to the road.

It had happened merely weeks ago. The pain of watching our house burn with my dad's body inside haunted my thoughts like dark shadows clinging to every simple moment. Each breath I took filled me with pain more powerful than the silver that was loath to leave my veins.

Chapter 15

My throat tightened and a sob wrenched from my battered heart, waking me from the haunted fever dreams. I tried to roll over, to curl in on myself in an effort to disappear completely, but realized my hands were tied. My heart raced with fear at the thought that perhaps Nikki's parents had gone back on their word. The chance to study an Alpha was too great to pass up.

"Jaze?"

Nikki's voice chased away the pain, the fear, and even the memories for the tiniest moment. For that instant, her nearness was my world. I clung to the familiar way she said my name as though we had been friends for years instead of weeks. I inhaled and fought to let her scent chase away the memories of blood, gasoline, and tainted smoke. Fingers touched my hair softly, afraid of hurting me. I ground my teeth to prevent the wry smile from reaching my lips. I had been so damaged both inside and out that even love at this point hurt.

"Jaze?"

I opened my eyes slowly, squinting in the light above the bed. A shadow blocked half of it from view. My eyes focused and the light faded to the background as the face took on detail. Nikki gazed down at me, her beautiful blue eyes bright with worry. A few strands of long black hair fell near her face and whispered across my chest. She looked so perfect, so absolutely perfect and pure and innocent and untouched by the cruelties of the world that I could only stare. I wondered why she dared touch me, and was afraid that the taint of the shadows I carried with me would cross over to her. My breath caught in my chest.

"Jaze, are you okay?" she asked softly, concern rising in her voice. "Are you here?"

"What do you mean?" I managed to croak out past my dry throat.

She smiled then so sweetly that it took my breath away. "You've been talking in your dreams, calling out to people I don't know, to your dad." Her voice dropped off as though she was afraid she had said too much.

I closed my eyes, then opened them again. "Hunters killed my dad just over a month ago."

Nikki's eyes widened and I saw my reflection in the tears that filled them. "Oh, Jaze. I'm so sorry. I'm so very sorry." She shook her head and wiped at the tears.

I wanted to touch her face, to tell her she didn't need to cry, but my hands were still tied to the table. "It's not your fault. You don't have to cry for me," I said, willing myself not to break down.

She cupped a palm to my face, her touch so soft I barely felt it. She leaned closer so that her eyes stared right into mine. She whispered, her lips an inch above mine, "You took all this pain for me. You saved my life. I owe you the world and I *will* cry for you."

"Because I'm so charming?" I forced out past the knot in my throat.

She gave a soft laugh. Her tears fell onto my cheeks and she leaned down and kissed me so softly yet so full of love that I couldn't hold in my emotions anymore.

I closed my eyes as my tears coursed down the sides of my face to linger in my hair. Nikki rested her cheek against mine and just held me while I cried, my heart and my soul so exposed and vulnerable she could have crushed me with a single word or look. I tried not to care, and hoped she would take what was left of me and destroy it. But deep down I wanted to live, I wanted to fight and stop Mason from hurting anyone else. I didn't want Dad's death to have been for nothing.

My sobs slowed and Nikki rose back up. She loosened the bands on my wrists and slipped them off. "My parents were afraid you'd hurt yourself further if you moved," she explained gently. I lifted up an arm and my body shook with the effort. My wrists were red and raw from the thrashing I had done during the silver fever. I definitely would have done more damage to myself if I hadn't been secured.

I sat up slowly, holding an arm across my stomach to ease the pain.

"I don't think you should be moving," Nikki said worriedly; her hands moved helplessly in the air as though she wanted to help, but didn't know how to without hurting me.

I gave her a weak smile. "It's okay, werewolves heal quickly." I slid slowly toward the side of the small cot, noticing for the first time that I was still in the gray-walled room that smelled of antiseptic and blood.

"Not werewolves wounded with silver," she argued, but when she saw I wouldn't be stopped, she ducked under one of my arms and supported me with her body.

"Where are your parents?" A shard of pain laced up my side from the knife wound and I gasped the last word. I held my stomach tightly. I could feel the stitches through the bandages that ran lengthwise across the front. It felt like my whole body was wrapped up. Too bad it wasn't Halloween, I could have passed for a mummy.

We walked through a door, down a hallway that smelled faintly of cat, and stopped at the doorway to the living room. Nikki's mom sat on the arm of a couch and her dad perched on the edge of an armchair, their heads close together as if they were in deep discussion. They both turned in surprise at our appearance. Meg blushed slightly and I realized they had been discussing me.

"Nikki, what are you guys doing?" she asked in alarm, rising to her feet.

I stepped into the room and Nikki helped me into the armchair opposite her dad. Her mom and dad both stared at me. "You should be resting," Meg pressed. There was genuine concern in her voice that I didn't want to hear.

"I need to know a couple of things," I forced out breathlessly at the ache in my ribs from the brief journey.

Her dad rose and checked my bandages. My instincts screamed at me to get as far away from the Hunters as I could, but I forced myself to hold still. I must have been too still because he gave me a strange look I couldn't read, but it was all I could do to keep from letting my fight or flight instincts take over.

He tut-tutted behind me in a fashion that was so doctorly and normal I could almost pretend he truly was a physician, but my instincts demanded for me to phase and tear them all apart, to end the danger to my life, my Mom's, Mouse's, and those of Chet's pack. I bit my lip and allowed him to proceed with his inspection. A few moments later he stepped back and gave a nod of satisfaction. "Everything seems to be healing, slowly, but healing. I've never seen a werewolf survive silver shards once they've reached the bloodstream. They have a nasty habit of heading straight for the heart." He glanced at his wife as if afraid he had gone too far. She pursed her lips and shook her head with a sigh. He shrugged and went back to sit by her.

Nikki settled on the couch closest to me, her eyes studying my face worriedly.

"What do you want to know?" Meg asked. At my guarded expression, her voice softened. "You deserve that much," she said.

I breathed in to clear my throbbing head, then gritted my teeth at the answering pain. "You hunt werewolves; you're Hunters," I said dryly.

Meg glanced at her husband as they both nodded together. Her eyebrows rose. "You already knew that?" she asked in surprise.

A sharp pain cut through my lacerated stomach. "Nikki told me," I forced out.

They both looked at Nikki. Her mom frowned in disapproval. "Darling."

"Don't darling me," Nikki cut her off angrily. "All you care about is killing werewolves. You don't even know I'm here half the time. Sorry for finding someone I could talk to before I exploded with the frustration of not feeling like I exist in my own home."

Her mother's eyebrows rose, but she replied blandly, "Another Alpha, really?"

Nikki blushed slightly. "I know, a little ironic, isn't it?"

A smile touched her dad's lips. He turned to me. "Fortunate."

I stared at him. He shrugged. "If Meg won't say it, I will. We owe you our daughter's life. We never thought Chet would react that way."

"Of course he reacted that way," I replied. "You hurt a member of his pack. A pack is a family, whether they're related or not. He responded the same way you did when a member of your family was killed."

They both looked taken aback at my strong words. I regretted them, but they had been said. I opened my mouth to soften the blow, but Nikki's father cut me off.

"You're right," he said softly. Nikki's mom set a hand on his arm, but he shook his head. "No, Meg. He is right. Nikki is, too. Ever since Randy died, we haven't been able to think of anything but killing werewolves. But they have lives, too, and families."

Meg's brow furrowed and I could tell she wanted to argue, but she pursed her lips and kept silent.

I shifted on the armchair in an effort to find a more comfortable position, but just moving hurt so I gave up. "I needed a friend as much as Nikki did. I was lucky she found me. Without her, I don't know what I would have done."

Nikki grabbed my hand and held it tight. Her mom frowned. "What are you talking about?" she asked, her tone more concerned than defensive now.

I held the words in limbo, feeling as if every time I said them made it more real. Finally, I sighed. "My dad was killed by Hunters." I breathed quickly, more spent than I wanted to admit. Dark spots danced before my eyes

Meg exchanged a glance with her husband. "How long ago was that?" he asked gently.

I closed my eyes in an effort to avoid the dancing spots, but they started to flash. A ringing began softly in my ears. "February 15th," I said. My words slurred slightly.

Nikki's mom let out her breath in a rush.

I swayed on the couch and it felt like the world moved in a circle around me. Nikki's hand tightened. "Roger, catch him. He's going to fall," Meg said quickly.

Strong arms caught me before I hit the ground. I was lifted up as though I didn't weigh more than a child. "You're gonna be fine, son. Just hang in there and we'll take care of you," Nikki's dad said in a calm, reassuring voice that sounded so much like my father's a sob caught in my chest. I faded to the rhythm of his footsteps down the hall.

"Jaze?"

I opened my eyes and was surprised to find Meg sitting on a chair next to the bed. She sighed and her eyes tightened with concern. "Jaze, I think I should call your mom and let her know what happened."

I shook my head, then put both my hands to my temples to stop the headache that threatened to split my skull. "No," I said between clenched teeth. "She's already been through too much."

Meg's concern showed in her voice. "You have, too. You need your mom."

I turned slightly so I could look at her. She sat on the chair Nikki usually occupied. She leaned forward with her elbows on her knees so that we were eye level. I cleared my throat. "She just lost her husband, relocated to a new city, had to find a new job, and has been working hard to provide for us. If she finds out that I went head to head with the local pack in an effort to save a Hunter's daughter, she'll never sleep again." I took a testing breath and was relieved when it hurt less than before. I let it out slowly. "She needs her sister right now and the kind of medicine being near family can bring. If she's here, all I'll do is worry about her safety and I won't be able to do what needs to be done."

Meg nodded slowly, her eyes a little bright.

A thought occurred to me and I tried to push up to a sitting position. She held me down with one hand, a feat which would have been impossible if I'd had my normal werewolf strength. I tried to rise again anyway. "I can go. If it's hard for you to have me here, I can leave. I understand and I'm grateful for all you've done."

Meg shook her head quickly. "I won't hear of it," she said firmly, cutting off my protests. "You're welcome to stay here as long as your mother is gone."

"I don't want to make things uncomfortable for you," I said. "I know werewolves killed your son."

"And Hunters killed your father," she replied.

I settled back on the bed and looked at her.

She met my eyes and gave a motherly smile. "We're quite the pair, aren't we?"

I nodded, my throat tight. The pain I felt echoed in her eyes. I swallowed and thought of something. "Do you know which werewolf you hurt?"

She frowned slightly as she thought, then shook her head. "It was one of the grays. We had our sights on Chet, but the gray got in the way. Our bullet hit it in the forearm; if they're smart and get the silver out quickly, it'll be fine."

I tried not to let show how much her talking of them like game animals bothered me. "How do you feel about that?"

"That I didn't kill it?" She gave me a searching look, a glint of humor in her eyes. "I was disappointed; now I'm not so sure. Roger's taken your words to heart. He seems to think it might be time to throw in the towel."

That surprised me. "How do you feel about it?"

She gave me a frank look. "Old habits die hard. I don't know what I'd do with myself."

A laugh escaped me and I grabbed my stomach when pain answered. "I'm sure you'll figure out something," I managed to get out. "Maybe keeping your daughter under control."

She laughed. "That would be a full time job."

"And she calls me a rebel," I said wryly.

Meg patted my shoulder. "You just take it easy and let those wounds heal. The more sleep you can get, the better." She gave me another motherly smile that made my heart ache, then rose and left the room.

A few seconds later Nikki came in with a bowl of

soup that smelled impossibly good. She scooted the chair closer to the bed. "Chicken noodle?" she asked with a smile.

"Yes, please," I answered. My mouth watered.

She scooped up broth and a few noodles with a spoon and tried to feed it to me. I laughed weakly. "I can feed myself," I said.

She shook her head. "Nope. He who risks his life for a girl gets pampered by said girl until he is fully recovered." I laughed again and clutched my stomach at the pain. "Is that a quote?"

She nodded. "Shakespeare, I think. Or maybe Elton John."

"Probably not Elton John," I said with a mouthful of soup.

She laughed. "Probably not. I might be misquoting."

"Might?"

She laughed louder this time and the sound healed my heart as much as her easy acceptance of my shattered soul. "Okay, definitely misquoting." She scooped up more soup and put it in my mouth before I could tease her further. Her forehead creased slightly. "You had a good talk with Mom?"

"She wanted to call my mom and tell her what happened," I said. At Nikki's concerned look, I shrugged. "Then she said I could stay here as long as I needed. Not what I expected from a pair of Hunters."

Nikki touched my shoulder. "You're not what I expected from a werewolf. I guess we've both got something to learn about judging before we truly know someone."

I nodded and settled into the comfortable silence we shared like a warm blanket. By the time the soup was gone, I could barely keep my eyes open. Nikki left me with a soft smile and promised she would be back when I woke up.

Chapter 16

"Maybe he could help us," Meg whispered from the next room. I eased out of the bed, relieved and surprised at how much better I felt after only a night.

"I don't know," Roger replied. "He's been through so much. We shouldn't press it."

I made my way down the hall and they both turned when I appeared. "Press what?" I asked. At Meg's frown, I pointed to my ears. "Can't help it. Werewolf, remember?"

Roger grinned, his eyes lighting up. "I didn't realize the attributes continued in human form. That's very interesting."

"And explains a lot," Nikki's mother said, exchanging a glance with him.

I shrugged. "Only some of them, and my hearing and eyesight aren't near as good in human form, just better than a human's."

Roger nodded as though noting that for later. I leaned against the arm of the couch to relax my sore muscles. "Ask me whatever you need to know."

Meg hesitated, glanced at Roger, then said, "We need to know why there aren't any Alphas in this area." She held up a hand at the concern on my face and rushed on, "Not that we want to kill them or anything, it's just that something's going on here and we need to figure it out."

Her words caught my attention. "So you've decided to give up the hunt?"

Meg's brow creased, but Roger smiled. "We've decided that we've thrown away too much of our lives trying to avenge Randy, when each wolf we kill gets us no closer to bringing him back." I heard Nikki's footsteps stop in the hall and was glad she heard. Roger continued, "We figure maybe we can be some sort of a liaison, you know, between werewolves and Hunters? Maybe we could stop some of the killing on both sides."

I stared at him and my heart pounded with the sincerity of his words. "You mean stop killing werewolves altogether?"

Meg nodded. "You're right about them, or you. You have families, mothers and fathers who care about you. What right do we have to kill you?" She shifted a little in her chair and dropped her eyes. "We almost killed that boy. We've always thought of them as animals, but it's come a little too close to home." She glanced toward the hall where Nikki stood out of sight.

I spoke my thoughts. "Well, there are werewolves who are out of line, dangerous ones who listen too much to instinct and not enough to their brains or conscience. Sometimes we can't handle them by ourselves before humans get hurt."

Roger jumped on that. "Maybe we could facilitate a sort of peace between the Hunters and werewolves. You know, work together and stuff!"

Meg and I both stared at him and I heard Nikki's sneakers shift on the carpet. "Are Hunters that organized?" I asked carefully. I had always pictured the werewolf-hating humans as individual lunatics with a thirst for wolf blood, not an organized and controlled group of killers. The thought was as scary as it was reassuring.

Roger nodded. "The Hunters are very organized. There's a central hub where all Hunter activities are monitored and where we receive our assignments; they know roughly how many werewolves live in each area and send us out in task forces for control situations." He stopped and glanced at Meg.

"Mass genocide," I said quietly. "Not pretty, but smart. Especially if they think what they're doing is for the common good."

"But they just don't know," Meg replied, her tone gentle.

I nodded and took a breath to rein in my emotions. "We'll deal with that later." I turned back to Roger. "You asked what was going on with the Alphas. It probably fits in with how the Hunters think we all are." I shook my head and continued, "My uncle, Mason, is in the process of killing all the Alphas in the hope of controlling their wolves. As far as I can tell, he wants power over all the North American packs. He's not an Alpha himself, but if he wipes out all of the Alphas, he'll be the next in line."

They stared at me, eyes reflecting their shock. Meg spoke, "We've got to tell the others."

Roger and I both shook our heads at the same time. Nikki took a few more steps down the hall until she stood just out of sight. "They'd bring Hunters to kill all the werewolves, not just the ones involved," I stated firmly. "There are innocent werewolves who deserve to live peaceful lives."

Meg snorted, but I could tell the derision was a habit. I pressed on, "What I need is your help to find Mason's home base so that I can defeat him and end the killing."

"And all the wolves will just go quietly back to their homes?" Meg asked with doubt heavy in her voice.

She frowned when I nodded. "As organized as Hunters seem to be, I'm guessing we come out on top when it comes to listening to Alphas. What Mason is doing is wrong, but because he's the strongest wolf around thanks to his killing spree, no one can challenge him."

Roger studied me. "But you can."

I nodded. "I can and I will. What he's doing is horrible and I'm going to put an end to it one way or another. I can't let him hurt anyone else."

Meg's voice grew gentle. "He had something to do with how your father died, didn't he?"

I nodded and clenched my fists to control the rage the thought brought to the surface. When I could trust my voice again, I forced out, "Yet another reason I don't want Mom involved in any of this."

"She's not a werewolf though, is she?" Meg asked.

I shook my head and ignored the way my chest constricted at the relief in her eyes. "She's not. It's a fluke I'm an Alpha, but we'll use it to our advantage." Meg and Roger glanced at each other, and Meg nodded. "We owe it to Nikki to help out however we can. We let her get involved in this and didn't realize she was in too deep until it was almost too late." She blinked the sudden shine of tears from her eyes. "We owe you for saving her life, and she won't be out of danger until things are settled."

I heard Nikki step around the corner and turned when her parents did. "I want in, too."

"No," her mother said. "It's too dangerous."

Nikki shook her head. "You're always leaving me out of everything. I can help and I want to this time."

Her father rose and took her hand, his eyes softening. "Nikki, darling, we just don't want you to get hurt."

She pulled her hand from his and I could hear from the way she breathed that she was fighting back tears. "A little late for that, Dad." She saw the pain in his eyes and touched his arm. "It's not like I'm asking to be thrown into the middle of a werewolf battle, but if I can help somehow, I want to be included."

Roger hesitated, then nodded despite the stubborn look on his wife's face. "We'll include you. Just promise you'll be careful."

Nikki nodded. "I promise."

Roger took a deep breath, and then turned to me. "Alright, where do we begin?"

***

It took another day before I felt well enough to sit through school, and one more before Nikki's mom agreed to let me. She didn't want any of us where Mason could find us unexpectedly, but I had to go. Alpha instinct wouldn't let me lie low when the safety of my loved ones was at stake. I had to speak to Chet to tell him about Mason's intentions and also to see if I could keep him from lashing out at Nikki and her family.

We sat around the table that morning and I could feel Meg's worry tight in the air. "I'll go by myself," I said for the twentieth time. "I can take care of it."

Nikki pointed her waffle-laden fork at me. "You're not going alone and you know it, so stop saying that."

Roger nodded. "You'll both be alright as long as you keep your weapons handy and your wits about you."

Meg rolled her eyes. "I still don't understand why you have to go. If Chet thinks he won, he'll leave you alone, right?"

My hands clenched into fists at the thought of Chet thinking he had beat me when he had used his whole pack to do it and still failed. I willed my hands to relax and took a calming breath. "I have to face Chet and tell him about his parents, and I have to show him that he didn't hurt me." Meg's eyebrows lifted and I fought back a grimace. "At least as much as I can hide. I'll call for Alpha Accord. He'll have to talk to me then."

"What's Alpha Accord?" Roger pressed.

I wondered how many laws I had broken by mentioning it, but it was too late and the laws hadn't protected my family so my respect of them was dwindling rapidly. I rubbed the back of my neck and winced when the movement pulled at my healing wounds. "It's a meeting between two Alphas.

When an Alpha calls for Alpha Accord, no other werewolf is allowed to touch him until he and the Alpha speak. After that, it's up to the Alpha in charge of the pack to decide what he wants to do."

"So he could have his wolves attack you?" Meg asked, concern in her voice.

I nodded, but didn't let the worry I felt show. "He won't after he's heard what I have to say. I need him on my side and I need to get to him before Mason does. The longer I wait, the more innocent lives are at stake."

Meg sighed, but knew if I wanted to leave the house, they couldn't stop me. "Alright, but you have your knives and the guns?"

I gritted my teeth, but nodded. Meg and Roger had taken Mason's methods to the next step, coating break-away silver knives in a silver-based gel to immediately slow any werewolves we used them on. They had also given us small pistols with silver bullets that we each carried in our backpacks. All of the weapons were cased in a specially formulated plastic that would hide the metal from the metal detectors at school. It felt like overkill to me, but I couldn't argue against parents protecting their daughter from a pack of angry werewolves.

It felt funny listening to Meg and Roger, but I owed them my life and the fact that they were willing to help still felt like a crazy dream. My stomach and side ached from the slowly healing knife wounds, but I had more energy and my strength was returning. I had spoken to Mom a few times on the phone. She was worried when she couldn't reach me the first day after the attack, but when I explained the neighbors had convinced me to stay at their place, she was thrilled. I just failed to mention it was because I had been ripped apart by werewolves. I felt guilty but knew it was better this way.

The doorbell rang and I jumped even though I had listened to the footsteps up the stairs. I pushed down the anxiety building in my chest and rose, pretending not to notice the glances Meg and Roger exchanged. Brock met Nikki and I at the front door with a big grin.

"I knew you were alive!" he exclaimed and gave me a punch on the shoulder that woke up the ache in my muscles from the silver poisoning. He threw his arms around me and hugged me tight.

I finally shrugged him off, embarrassed but happy to see him, too. "Well, someone had to protect you on your walks to school. How did you manage when I was gone?" My tone was only teasing on the surface.

Brock grinned. "I told my mom I was sick. She let me stay home and play video games. Best sickness ever."

Nikki and I laughed. I moved to sling my backpack over my shoulder, but Brock grabbed it from me. "I'll get that."

"Hey!" I protested.

Brock shook his head. "You should be dead after what you've been through. The last thing you need is to be hauling a heavy load of books to school." He shook the backpack with a suspicious look. "Although this is surprisingly light."

I laughed again but the pain that laced through my stomach stole my breath. "You know I don't study," I managed to get out. I leaned against Nikki's porch railing for support.

Brock grinned, but I could see the worry in his eyes. He slung the backpack over one shoulder. "Well, I suppose I should be grateful you don't want to pass your junior year."

"Watch it," I said with mock anger.

"Whatcha gonna do? Breathe on me?" he teased. I grabbed for him and he danced just out of reach. "Uh-huh, just what I thought. I guess I'll be protecting you on the way to school."

I grimaced and followed him down the sidewalk, Nikki at my side. The knives strapped to my ankle felt conspicuous and strongly out of place, but their weight was reassuring given the exhaustion that refused to leave my body. I felt a surge of gratitude that Meg had fashioned the knife holster so that the silver wouldn't touch my skin.

By the time we reached the school, I regretted not taking one more day to help my body recover. When we entered the front doors, the smell of silver from all the students making their way through the metal detectors hit me full force. I breathed out of my mouth and fought back a wave of nausea. I glanced at Brock and he shouldered past me. "I got this," he whispered as he went by.

Brock dropped some silver wristbands, a couple rings, and two silver chains into two separate cups, discreetly handed me one, then passed his to the security guard as he went through the metal detector. I did the same, took my cup on the other side, and slipped it back to him with a sigh of relief. Even being that close to silver made my skin crawl. Brock gave me a thumbs-up and tossed the contents of both cups into his backpack.

Members of Chet's pack stared at us as we made our way down the hall. Nikki walked so close to me our shoulders touched, but the werewolves didn't seem to notice her. I met their shocked gazes until they remembered protocol and dropped their eyes. Several wore slings and bandages, and Shane, one of the smaller members of the pack, had a splint from his elbow to his wrist from Meg's bullet. I felt like a weight lifted off my shoulders knowing he had survived being shot and I smiled despite his glare. The pack took off down the hall together and I knew we wouldn't catch Chet by surprise. His anticipation of our arrival could make things a bit harder, but it was too late to turn back now.

Mouse leaned against my locker and his eyes lit up when he saw us walking down the hall. I patted his shoulder in thanks and he grinned at me, pushing his glasses up on his nose. "You've walked into the lion's den," he whispered.

"I know, I planned on that," I told him. He nodded, his eyes worried. I threw my mostly empty backpack in the locker, then Mouse, Nikki, and Brock followed me toward the side hall where Chet and his pack hung out.

"You're meeting him now?" Brock asked; he fought to keep his voice down.

"Better now than later," I said. He looked around me at Nikki, but I pretended not to notice and kept walking, leaving them to catch up or fall behind. I fought to keep my breath steady, alarmed at how quickly my returning strength wavered, but I forced any sign of weakness or pain down when I rounded the corner.

Most of Chet's pack stood around him with their backs to us. After a few steps down the hall, the closest wolves smelled me and turned. "What the-" Chet growled. Then he looked straight into my eyes. His gaze widened then narrowed. He glared at me. "What are you doing here?"

"We need to talk," I said. I was aware of the way his pack began to inch around my sides to get behind me. I heard the scuff of a shoe and Nikki, Mouse, and Brock were at my shoulders.

Chet shook his head. "Never."

I threw down the one law he couldn't break. "I demand Alpha Accord."

His brow lowered angrily and he gestured to the hallway. "Here?"

I pointed to the bathroom door. Max, his second in command, stepped into the bathroom. A slight scuffle ensued and two students rushed out and sped past us, throwing glances over their shoulders. He nodded at Chet.

"You first," Chet said with a dangerous gleam in his eyes.

I shrugged and pushed past his pack mates to enter the bathroom before him. My instincts screamed for me not to turn my back on him, and I had to remind myself that we had a common enemy, he just didn't know it yet. Whispers rose among his pack members before the bathroom door even shut. Worry for Nikki, Brock, and Mouse clouded my intentions, but Nikki was armed even better than myself, and both Meg and Roger attested to her skill with a firearm, yet another perk of being raised by werewolf Hunters.

"You're supposed to be dead," Chet growled as I turned to face him. He leaned with his back against the door in an effort to make me feel trapped.

I leaned against the opposite wall, grateful to take a little weight off my legs before they collapsed under me. If he knew how close his statement came to the truth, he might finish me off instead of talking. "It was a nice try," I said casually.

He frowned and pushed off the door, but I held up a hand. "Hear me out. You owe me that much."

He blew out his breath angrily, but leaned against the door again. I took that to be a good sign.

"There's more going on here than you know."

He bristled and his eyes darkened. "I have control of my pack, if that's what you're implying."

I shook my head. "That much is obvious. They definitely jump at your every command." Before he could get any angrier, I continued, "You tried to kill me, but I don't think it was really you who wanted me dead."

"I tried to kill Nikki," Chet countered, but his jaw twitched slightly at the statement as though it was hard to say.

"You just happened to get in the way."

I clenched my hands to keep from hitting him. "Why would you try to kill either of us?"

His own hands balled into fists and he shook with the attempt to control himself. "I found out her parents are Hunters."

I nodded. "I knew that, too, but that's no justification for trying to kill them."

Chet's eyes widened. "They kill werewolves, and unless you're okay with your pack members being slaughtered, you'd fight back, too."

My heart slowed and I met his eyes without challenge. "What if I told you it wasn't the Hunters behind some of the werewolf deaths." Chet's jaw clenched, but he didn't interrupt. I pushed on. "Have you stopped to think about the fact that every Alpha and older wolf in this pack has been killed in the last couple of years?"

He shook his head. "I'm the only Alpha in this pack."

"Now," I said quietly.

I watched him carefully. He studied me as he thought. I could almost see his mental track as he went through his parents, then the parents of his pack members, older siblings, and any relatives with werewolf blood. The color washed from his face and his glaring anger dissolved into shock. "What are you saying?" he finally asked in a strangled voice.

"I'm saying," I replied quietly, "Someone is systematically killing off anyone who could stand in the way of gaining control of the pack."

He took a step forward and I held up a hand. "Not me," I said firmly. "I had my own pack and I had to walk away just like you'll be forced to do if you want to save your life. We've got to put a stop to this."

Chet leaned back against the door, sliding down until he sat on the bathroom floor. I eased down on the opposite wall and stifled a sigh as my weary muscles relaxed. Chet held his head in his hands; his black hair fell to hide his face. I stayed quiet until he looked up at me. "Why would someone want my pack?"

"Not just your pack," I replied softly. "He wants every pack. As far as I can tell, he wants control of all the werewolves."

His eyes darkened. "Who?"

"Mason."

His hands clenched at the name; denial on his face slowly washed to horror. He shook his head, opened his mouth as if to argue, then closed it and rose to his feet. I kept perfectly still, hoping I would have the energy to fight back if it came to that. But he wasn't looking at me. It was as if I no longer existed in the tiny bathroom. A growl escaped Chet's lips and he grabbed the hand dryer and ripped it from the wall. He threw it against the bathroom stall and it bounced to the floor, leaving a big dent in the metal.

I chuckled.

Chet turned on me with a glare. "You want some of this?" His eyes flashed with anger.

I shook my head. "No. Actually, I did the same thing with that a few days ago. I was just wondering what the janitor's going to think when he comes in and finds it on the floor again."

Chet glared down at the hand dryer for a moment, and looked at the dent in the stall and the hole in the wall where a couple of forlorn wires poked out. He looked at me again and breathed out his frustrations in a half sigh, half chuckle. "You're alright, Jaze."

I let out a relieved laugh. "I tried to tell you that when we first met, but for some reason you wouldn't listen."

He slumped back to the floor against the door. The implications of what he had just learned looked heavily out of his eyes. "How do you know it's Mason?"

I met his gaze, knowing my own was just as haunted. "He's my uncle and he killed my father."

He stared at me for a minute, then nodded. "You're in deep."

I let out a breath. "I've got to stop this." I glanced at him. "You've got to promise me you won't try to take him on alone. I know you feel like you have to protect your pack, but he's done all the damage he can do for now until he gets to you. Going to him would be the last thing you should do."

He frowned and I could see he didn't like being told what to do. It was an Alpha thing. "You've got a plan?"

I nodded. "I'm going to organize the Hunters."

His mouth fell open at my bluntness, and he gave a dark chuckle. "You're bold."

I nodded. "I'm not about to fight nice."

He gave me an approving look. "I can respect that."

Chet pushed to his feet and offered me a hand. I took it gingerly and he pulled me up. "We got you a little worse than you're letting on, didn't we?"

I nodded and pulled up my shirt. Angry black streaks ran from the knife wound across my stomach and the one in my ribs. The wounds themselves had been sewn shut by Nikki's parents because they were healing so slowly. Meg would have preferred to staple them, but I couldn't take anymore metal in my body. I had taken the bandages off that morning, worried the werewolves would see their bulkiness and attack me when I was weak. A slight trickle of blood ran from the one across my stomach. I dropped my shirt back down.

Chet shook his head with a whistle. "Man, remind me never to get on your bad side."

I laughed wryly. "I was about to say the same thing about you."

He grinned and opened the door for me. We both walked back out to the waiting pack.

Chapter 17

Brock, Mouse, Nikki and I walked to Nikki's house after school. There was an unspoken agreement that we would stick together until things with Mason were resolved. Between the confrontation with Chet, sitting in hard chairs all day, and the walk home, I was ready to collapse. A surge of adrenaline ran through my veins when I saw both of Nikki's parents waiting for us on her front porch.

Brock and Mouse waited politely at the edge of the driveway, Mouse nervously eying the two Hunters as Nikki and I approached.

"How are you feeling, dear?" Meg asked. The worry she felt reflected in her eyes as she brushed the hair back from my face. Roger gave his daughter a hug.

"I'm fine. Things went well at school today." I said it casually, but they both knew what it meant. Their daughter was safe, for now at least. Meg and Roger exchanged a look of relief.

Roger cleared his throat. "You, uh, might want to spend the night next door. There might be some disagreeable people coming to visit, if you know what I mean."

Nikki's eyes widened. "You mean the Hunters are coming tonight?"

Meg sighed. "We're trying to be subtle, darling. And yes, they're coming tonight. We're hoping to talk them into meeting with Jaze tomorrow."

"Tomorrow!" Nikki looked at me with a mixture of surprise and fear.

I shrugged. "I'd rather have it over with sooner than later. We need to stop things quickly." I was glad I sounded confident despite the knot in my stomach at the thought of meeting with a group of werewolf killing Hunters.

The worry in Nikki's eyes was reflected on her parents' faces, but they nodded in agreement. I thanked them and we headed back to the empty house that was supposed to be my home. When I walked through the door, I felt only a rush of bitterness at all that had brought me there. I stifled a sigh and eased down on the thick carpet in the front room.

Brock flung himself on the couch, and Nikki took the easy chair. Brock scooted to make room for Mouse, but the werewolf merely shook his head and settled on the floor with his back against the couch. He picked up a ball of tape left over from unpacking boxes and began to toss it in the air.

After a couple of tosses, Brock leaned over and caught it on the way down. "You're really a werewolf?"

Mouse shrugged, but his cheeks reddened.

Brock shook his head in astonishment. "All this time?"

Mouse gave a sheepish grin. "It's not like I suddenly became one overnight."

"I know," Brock said, "It's just, you know." He gestured vaguely with the ball.

"Unexpected?" Nikki filled in helpfully.

He nodded, then pointed at me. "And you knew!"

I nodded. "That first day in the lunchroom."

"And you didn't say anything?"

I tipped my head at Mouse. "He asked me not to."

"When?" Brock asked. "I didn't hear anything."

"It wasn't in so many words," I said. Brock shook his head again and fell silent.

"So, what do you want to do?" he asked after a couple more minutes.

I tipped my head to look at Nikki and smiled. "How about some street hockey?"

She stared at me in surprise. "There's no way you can play."

"Play?" Brock turned to Mouse. "What are they talking about?"

"No idea," he replied with a shrug. He looked at me questioningly.

I raised an eyebrow. "You mean you've never been tempted to go out after curfew and see what rebellious kids do when we're bored?"

Mouse shook his head. "Hard enough avoiding the pack during the day, let alone at night."

I gave him a reassuring smile. "Don't worry. Chet and I have an agreement. We'll be fine." I glanced outside at the slowly setting sun. "We just have to find something to do until nightfall."

***

Brock convinced us to play a card game he called Spat after a lot of persuading. It was fast and required way more energy than I had, so I eventually sat out and watched Nikki school them and take all of their cards. By the time they were done, Brock grudgingly gave Nikki the prized Twinkie they had played for and I paced the floor, anxious to be out of the house. I led the way through the back door and paused by the fence.

"You're going to rip your stitches," Nikki warned. "Mom'll be upset."

I grinned at her. "For some reason, that just doesn't scare me like it might have a few days ago." I grabbed the top of the fence and levered myself over. The stitches definitely pulled and hurt, but seemed to hold just fine as I dropped to the weeds and grass beyond.

"Oh, just wait," Nikki warned. "You haven't seen her angry."

Brock laughed and jumped over after me with Mouse close behind. Nikki shook her head and followed.

The toll of the day made me pace myself and it was well beyond nightfall by the time we made it to the abandoned mall parking lot.

"Hold on," Brock whispered. He grabbed my arm. "There's a security guard."

"It's okay," I said. I made my way toward Mr. Sathing, glad to see he was back on duty.

"He's a friend of ours," Nikki explained as the others followed reluctantly behind.

"You're friends with a parking lot patrolman?" Brock whispered. "What have you two been up to?"

Nikki laughed quietly and hurried to catch up.

"Go home, it's not safe out here," Mr. Sathing called; his voice cracked slightly. He shined his flashlight at us and the color returned to his cheeks. "Oh, it's you two. Haven't I told you to be careful?"

I nodded and shook his hand. "Yes, sir. Thank you again for the warning. We're escorting these two students so they don't get into any trouble."

Mr. Sathing's brow creased thoughtfully and he shone the flashlight at Brock and Mouse, studying them up and down carefully as though storing them in his memory. He finally nodded and turned back to me. "Good to see you're being responsible."

Nikki flashed me a bewildered smile and I knew she also wondered how sneaking out after curfew to hang out with a bunch of other high school students would be considered responsible, but I shrugged. "Sure thing. You take care of yourself."

"You, too," he said.

We had walked about halfway across the parking lot when he called my name. "Hey, Jaze?"

"Be right back," I said to the others.

I turned and jogged slowly back to the security guard.

"Yes, sir?"

He glanced at the others to make sure they were far enough away not to overhear. He then lowered his voice. "I couldn't make it to the meeting tonight, but even so, I'm sure they'll give you a listening to."

I stared at him, my heartbeat quickening. "You're a Hunter?"

He nodded. "Had an ex-wife that turned out to be a werewolf. Orneriest woman you ever saw. Thought it was just a time of the month thing." His cheeks reddened. "Turns out it was a different time of the month thing."

I frowned. "So you turned Hunter?"

Sadness filled his eyes. "She took my kids away. Said she had to raise them in a pack. Becoming a Hunter was the only way I could protect them from the others."

My heart tightened and I glanced up at the waning moon. It shone through a thin cloud cover, creating a rainbowed ring through the gray. I took a deep breath. "I'm sorry. If I ever meet your kids, I'll keep an eye on them."

He nodded and turned. I put a hand on his shoulder and he stopped. "You knew I was a werewolf the first time we met?"

He shrugged and avoided my gaze. "Had my suspicions. But you didn't seem to be up to anything bad."

I studied him curiously. "So why all the talk about werewolves?"

He smiled. "Just testing the waters. You never know who you can trust out here."

I nodded and let him go, then had a thought. "Hey, what're your kids' names?"

"Darryl and Max," he called out over his shoulder without turning.

I froze, and then sighed. Of course they would be members of Chet's pack. I hurried to catch up to the others.

I was exhausted by the time we reached the fenced swap meet. Mouse helped me lever Nikki and Brock over, then offered his interlaced fingers to me with a questioning glance. At my look he dropped his eyes. "I just thought. . . ."

It was against my instincts to show weakness, but we both knew I wouldn't make it over the fence by myself. I swallowed my pride and nodded. "Thanks, man." I stepped into his hands. He smiled and levered me up to the top. I turned and dropped to the other side, then stumbled slightly when I hit the ground.

Brock grabbed my arm to steady me. "You okay?"

I nodded but could tell by the look in his eyes that he didn't believe me. "I'll take it easy," I reassured him. He nodded, unconvinced.

"I still don't know what we're doing here," he said; he glanced around uneasily between the locked stalls. A whoop followed by a cheer sounded in the distance. His eyebrows rose.

"Come on." Nikki laced her arm through mine and we led the way down the aisle.

We stepped into the lit-up end alley and waited for Brock and Mouse to pass us. They both stopped and stared.

"Whoa," Mouse said quietly.

"Awesome!" Brock crowed. A group of roller skaters passed us, the puck a blur between them. Several other students ran by with a football. One student threw it and two more jumped to hit it out of the air. One managed to swat it down; it bounced off one of the stalls and fell at Brock's feet.

"Throw it," a student a few years younger than us said, gesturing toward three students by the hockey goal.

"They play both games at the same time?" Mouse asked me quietly.

I shrugged. "I guess it makes it more of a challenge."

Brock threw the ball in a wobbly spiral, then glanced at Mouse. "Come on, man! This is what we've been waiting for!"

"We have?" Mouse questioned; he glanced from me to the mad rush of roller skaters that almost took out the football players.

Brock nodded enthusiastically. "Yeah, we just didn't know it. Let's go!" He pushed off the wall and ran down the aisle, leaving Mouse to follow.

"Like kids in a candy shop," Nikki noted with a smile.

I nodded. "Got to let out steam somewhere."

"So, where to for us?"

"You're not heading out there?" I tipped my head toward the pile of skaters. Brock had managed to trip up the entire team and they now untangled themselves with an enthusiasm that made me tired just watching.

Nikki shook her head. "If you're not, I'm not."

I gave her a smile of gratitude. "What do you want to do?"

She pointed to one of the low rooftops. Students lined the sides, throwing wrappers and empty cans at the skaters and football players below. "How about up there?"

I shrugged. "Sounds good." We made our way to the far end. It took some effort to get to the top and by the time we were settled I had to fight to catch my breath. It felt good to finally stop moving.

Nikki leaned against me and we watched the students below. Mouse had the football, but a dozen guys charged at him. He ducked at the last second and dove right under the legs of the first guy, then knocked down the rest of them like bowling pins. The football slid out and was scooped up by someone else. Three guys, Brock included, stopped and helped everyone up. He and Mouse laughed despite the bruises and rushed off to catch up with the group. They barely missed the group of skaters that rushed by after the puck. One hit the puck just as another tipped his skate with a hockey stick. They got tangled and the group fell over in a heap as the puck slid into the goal at the far end.

A long forgotten memory surfaced. I tipped my head back against the metal roof and closed my eyes.

Dad pulled on a pair of silver and black roller skates while I tied my yellow and black ones. The bow wouldn't hold tight enough, and after he got his on he knelt and tied mine for me. I sat at the edge of a fountain. Water normally spilled down from the mouths of the four horses that stood on their hind legs, but it had been turned off for the night. Coins winked like twinkling stars in the clear water.

Dad held out a hand.

"You two be careful!" Mom cautioned from a bench. She waved the book she was reading at us for emphasis.

Dad nodded. "Don't worry, it can't be that hard!"

He pulled me up with a yank that sent us both sprawling on the ground. We laughed and rose shakily to our feet. Mom stood now, her expression worried and motherly. I smiled at her. "Don't worry, Mom," my eight-year-old self said. "It takes more than a couple falls to break us."

She mumbled something that sounded like, "It'd better," before she settled back on the bench and pretended to read her book.

Dad's knees wobbled a bit, but he soon found his balance. I fought to keep my ankles straight despite the tight laces.

Dad frowned. "We'd better get you better skates."

I shrugged. "These are fine, I've just got to get the hang of it."

Dad's eyes creased at the corners and he watched my ankles wobble back and forth for a second, then his eyes lit up. "I have an idea!"

He skated back to the car, dug around in the trunk for a moment, then brought back a roll of something gray.

"What are you doing?" Mom questioned suspiciously.

Dad held up the roll. "Duct tape. It fixes everything!"

He knelt down and proceeded to wrap the tape tightly around my roller skates. By the time he was done I didn't wobble an inch. "This is great!" my young self shouted. I pushed off and skated around the fountain.

CHEREE ALSOP

"Come on, Jaze. Let's go!" Dad said. He took off down the moonlit sidewalk and I followed close behind.

Chapter 18

"Jaze, you okay?"

The memory vanished and I shook my head to clear it. Nikki looked over at me, her face anxious. I nodded. "Just thinking."

"You looked so sad," she said.

I shrugged, fighting back the tightness in my chest. "Just remembering my first time roller-skating. My Dad taught me."

She fell silent and put her forehead against my shoulder for a minute. When she spoke, her voice was muffled against my shirt. "I'm so sorry about your Dad, Jaze."

I ran a hand down her long black hair. "He was a great guy."

"He had to be," she said. She looked up at me, her eyes bright.

I nodded. "He was the best dad ever." I smiled, remembering. "It wasn't always easy. Two Alphas in the house lead to some pretty interesting squabbles, but I always knew he loved me and he was there any time I needed him." I took a deep breath to push the pain away.

Nikki squeezed my arm, then leaned up and kissed me on the cheek.

"Hey, Jaze!" Brock shouted from below.

I growled under my breath which made Nikki smile. She turned and peered down the aisle. "What's up, Brock?"

"I, uh. . . " I swear I could actually hear him blushing. "The, uh, game's over. It's probably time to head outta here."

Nikki threw me a purse-lipped smile which meant that she knew the effects she had on him. She leaned back over. "Okay, we'll be down in a sec."

She rose and pulled me to my feet. I protested. "It's comfortable here. Let's just stay."

She shook her head. "Not if the nasty werewolves can get us."

"Hey!" I said.

She laughed and jumped down, then offered me a hand. I brushed it away and eased off the roof. "I'm not that feeble," I said. I let go and dropped. The impact at the bottom stole my breath away with jarring pain from my ribs and stomach. I leaned against the wall in an attempt to look nonchalant.

She leaned beside me. "I know you're not," she said with a look in her eyes that said I wasn't fooling her.

After I caught my breath, we followed the others back over the fence. The walk home felt shorter, and I was glad to find my strength returning. If only Mason knew what opportunity he was missing by not attacking me now.

**

We walked Brock and Mouse home as much for safety as for the company. It felt nice to be in a pack again, even if that pack was made up of one skinny werewolf, a Hunter's daughter, and an overly-enthusiastic, protective friend.

I walked Nikki to her fence, but stopped her before she could climb over. She looked at me. "What's wrong, Jaze?"

I hesitated, then spoke the thought that had circled through my mind during the walk. "When was the last time you went on a date? A real date, not just a hang-out with some werewolf jock?"

She smiled. "You are a werewolf jock."

My smile fell and I looked down at the ground, regretting my words. She put a hand on my shoulder and waited until I looked at her. "If this is your way of asking me out," she said softly, "Then I would be delighted."

I studied her expression to see if she was teasing, but she was more serious than I had ever seen her. I smiled. "Okay, tomorrow at eight o'clock we'll go on a date, a real date."

"Where are we going?"

I shrugged. "Haven't figured that part out yet."

She smiled again and hugged me tight. I stood there surprised and still until she let go, threw me one last smile, then climbed over the fence.

I waited until her back door slid shut, then gingerly lifted myself over my fence and down the other side. I walked slowly through the yard to the empty house, tapping the punching bag with my knuckles in passing. Before I could reach my back door, Nikki's door slid open again. I looked over, expecting to see her there, but instead made out Roger's form in the light that pooled from their kitchen.

"Jaze? You there, son?"

My heart clenched at being called son. It took me a minute to speak up. "Yes, sir?"

"The meeting's set," he said. "Tomorrow at six a.m."

I took a steeling breath. "I'll be there."

I touched the door, but he spoke again. "And Jaze?"

I turned back at the change in his tone. "Sir?"

He sighed. "It's not going to be easy."

"I know." The dread I had fought away all evening came back with full force. A room full of Hunters, all of which had probably killed werewolves, would be waiting to meet with me, one lone, unarmed, already injured werewolf. Roger nodded and went back inside. I took a last breath of the humid night air and did the same. The shutting of the sliding door sounded final, as though it locked away a part of my life I would never find again. It was the same feeling I had had when I flicked the cigarette lighter to set our house on fire after Dad was killed. I wondered what part of my life had been taken away by Hunters this time.

***

I went to the Valen's house at five o'clock the next morning. Nikki met me at the door with circles under her eyes as though she hadn't slept well. I knew I looked the same way. Roger and Meg met us in the living room and we waited almost patiently for the inevitable.

It was nearly six when Roger pulled a paper grocery bag out from behind the couch. "They have a few stipulations for the meeting," he said apologetically. The embarrassment in his tone was unmistakable.

I nodded, expecting as much. "Okay, what are they?"

He withdrew a cloth bag that tightened around the bottom with drawstrings. "The first is that you be hooded so that you can't see where the meeting is held."

I fought back a smile. It was not like I would want to go back there anyway. "Okay, and?"

He hesitated and Meg took the bag from him. "You have to be restrained," she said, pulling out a pair of handcuffs.

"What?" Nikki stood. "Mom, that's ridiculous. They're handcuffing him, one werewolf with who knows how many armed Hunters? That's not fair!" She glanced at me, fear for my life showing in her eyes.

I caught her hand. "It'll be okay. If it makes them feel safer, I can take it." She stared at me and I smiled encouragingly. "I'm just lucky they granted this meeting in the first place."

"I don't think luck had anything to do with it," she muttered, but she sat down next to me again.

I stood and put my arms behind my back. When Meg fastened the handcuffs a jolt of pain ran up my arms. I glanced back at her in surprise. "Silver, really?"

She nodded. "I'm sorry, Jaze. I really am. They insisted." She leaned closer and whispered as though other Hunters were close enough to hear. "But these are just plated, so hopefully they won't do much damage."

I sat again on the edge of the couch, my arms tingling.

Nikki refused to speak, her hatred for the situation evident on her face.

I listened to the car pull up, a trio of footsteps walk up the sidewalk, and heard them stop for a moment at the porch. A few seconds later, at exactly six o'clock, a knock sounded at the door.

Roger sighed. "Well, here we go." He placed the cloth bag over my head and drew the strings closed, then took my arm and helped me up. It was awkward with my hands behind my back and I hoped there wouldn't be much rising and sitting at the meeting.

The door opened and three different footsteps entered the room.

"Is that it?" one of the Hunters asked coldly.

"This is Jaze Carso," Meg replied firmly. I smiled at her defiance.

I took a step toward the door.

"Wait!" Nikki jumped up from the couch and pulled the hood off my head. She rose on her tiptoes and kissed me on the lips. I closed my eyes against the pounding of my heart. One of her hands rested against my chest, and I could feel the heat radiating off it. I wondered if she felt my heartbeat.

The kiss was over quicker than I wanted it to be, but the taste lingered on my lips. "For good luck!" she said, out of breath. A blush stole across her cheeks and she returned to the couch without meeting her parents' eyes.

Roger let his breath out in a rush and picked up the hood she had discarded on the floor. He met my eyes briefly, his expression unreadable as he slipped the hood back over my head.

The footsteps backed up and we walked out the door. Roger guided me down the steps and the sidewalk and I ducked into a car that smelled of peppermint, gun oil, hand sanitizer, and amusingly, crayons, which attested that we were driving in a family car not accustomed to chauffeuring handcuffed werewolves. There was also one other occupant, the driver, who smelled of starch, hand soap, and hair care products.

"Let's go," the first voice growled.

The trip felt longer than necessary with an excess of stops, turns, and roundabouts. When the door opened and I smelled the myriad of scents on the humid morning air, I realized we hadn't even left the city. I fought back a grim chuckle at their pathetic attempt to disorient me.

Roger took my arm again and this time Meg walked on the other side, her hand resting gently on my forearm. "It's going to be okay," she said under her breath, but her voice quivered slightly, betraying her fears.

We walked up cement steps and entered through doors that smelled of old planks and decay. A warehouse. Our footsteps echoed on the cracked wooden floor. We crossed a small room that smelled of sawdust and mice, then another door was pulled open and we entered a much bigger area. Air flowed as though through open windows, and the talking of at least forty people stopped at our entrance.

My heart slowed and a cold pit formed in my stomach. They had gathered together more Hunters than I would have thought possible in such a short time. Again, the implications of organization tore away all of my preconceived thoughts about Hunters. I pushed the feeling away, reminding myself that more Hunters would be welcomed and needed in this fight.

We walked to the middle of the room and turned to face the waiting audience. Roger squeezed my arm and took a few steps away. "You'll be okay, sweetie," Meg whispered on my other side. She patted my elbow and made her way to Roger. They both went to join the others.

They sat, clothes rustling, and a deep silence fell. I waited as patiently as I could. I counted the seconds in my head until five minutes ticked by. The adrenaline from our entrance faded and the ache in my stomach and ribs began to rise. I shifted my feet, frustrated at their lack of courtesy. Scents of anger, hostility, and a hint of fear flowed from the group and through my hood.

Underneath it I could make out the scents of occupation, the bread, soap, and fruit-laced perfume smell of a housewife, the ink, electronic, stale scent of office workers, the sawdust and metal smell of a construction worker, the grease and oil scent of mechanics, the old paper and slightly mildewed carpet smell of a librarian, the antiseptic scent of several employed in the medical field, the dry-erase marker and sharpened pencil smell of the school teacher, and many others I worked to place to maintain my patience.

I wondered briefly how they had all gotten off work, then realized this was intended to be a short meeting, scheduled early in the morning so they could go to their jobs afterward. It showed that they didn't give much importance to the reason of this meeting, betting that it would be over within the hour.

"What is this?" I asked, fighting to keep my tone polite.

"You will wait until spoken to," someone spat out.

"Rensh, that isn't necessary," a deeper voice corrected him.

The nerves of being surrounded by obviously hostile Hunters and the odds that at least one pair here had probably been responsible for my Dad's death made my muscles ache. I longed to phase and show them what I really thought about standing cuffed and blind. Another minute passed. My legs wobbled slightly with the effort to stand; I forced them to hold and concentrated on breathing deeply. "Are we going to talk or am I just to stand here?" I asked, gritting my teeth to keep from shouting.

"We're waiting for one more person," the deep voice said; I could hear his dislike at answering a werewolf.

The outside door opened, two pairs of footsteps entered, crossed the small room, then opened the inside door. Clothes rustled as though gestures were made, and the pair crossed the room and sat near Roger and Meg. Their scent wafted past me and my blood turned cold as images of blood, pain, and the musky woods scent of my dad mixed with it. They were two of the Hunters responsible for his death.

The deep voice spoke. "We will hold this impromptu meeting with order." He said it loud enough for everyone to hear, but his head was turned toward me alone. "You will speak when spoken to, and will conduct yourself as humanly as possible."

Roger cleared his throat.

"That is uncalled for," Meg said, the anger in her voice barely under control.

A gavel struck wood and the voice spoke again. "Megan Valen, you will obey the rules of this meeting or you will be dismissed."

"Yes, sir," Meg replied, her voice muffled as though she bowed her head.

The deep voice turned back to me. "It isn't entirely clear why this meeting has been called in the first place. The Valens only said that it was urgent and life threatening. That we even allow you to participate is an honor no other werewolf has been granted."

"I feel honored," I muttered under my breath.

"What was that?" he demanded.

I bit back a reply and closed my hands into fists behind my back.

He sighed and hit the gavel again. "This meeting is called to order. We now grant the werewolf two minutes to state its business."

I turned toward his voice, feeling stupid with the bag over my head but worried about angering him enough to stop the meeting altogether. I had no delusions that I would be allowed out alive if things didn't go well. I cleared my throat. "Sir, a werewolf is killing off the Alphas in order to take control of the packs himself."

I waited a minute for my words to sink in, and was startled when he began to laugh, a deep, throaty chuckle that lifted the hair on the back of my neck. "And we're supposed to be concerned about a werewolf killing off other werewolves?" Several others in the audience laughed with him. "That's good for us."

My lips pulled back in a snarl and I fought to maintain control. "You don't understand," I forced out slowly, my words deep with the anger in my chest. "If he succeeds, you will have one werewolf in charge of all of the North American wolves. It would be a disaster for everyone."

"Oh?" he questioned, still chuckling. "And why is that?"

"Do you know why wolves in the wild keep their pack numbers small?" I asked, barely concealing the hostility in my voice at his amusement.

He sighed, his voice still laced with humor. "Do explain."

My legs tingled, restless to change with the rage-filled adrenaline coursing through my veins. I took a step in his direction and heard him step back. "It's detrimental to the pack. There's not enough food, and control is too hard to maintain. Large packs require bigger territories. Wolf packs, like the werewolf ones, are limited to family members with one or two exceptions. That's how it's supposed to be."

"So we just kill the leader and everything is taken care of," he concluded blatantly.

I shook my head. "It's never that easy." The hood was starting to really annoy me; it brushed my lips when I spoke and muffled my voice to those listening. The bite of the silver in the cuffs was just one more jab of humiliation.

"And why not?" he pressed with an annoyed tone.

"Because-" I couldn't take it anymore. I flexed my forearms behind me and broke the chain between the handcuffs, then ripped the bag from my head and threw it down.

Hunters who had been seated in metal chairs stood in alarm and backed up until they hit the chairs of those behind them. The one with the deep voice stood closest to me behind a makeshift podium. He was a dark-skinned, dark-eyed man who was overweight and wore a yellow sash with two blue stripes across his chest. He glared at me angrily. A gun from a holster on his hip now rested in his hand.

I twisted my left cuff and tore it from my wrist, then did the same to the right. Angry red burns showed where they had been, my body's reaction to even plated metal while the remnants of the silver from my wounds was in my body. I threw the cuffs down to the floor; they bounced once and stopped with a metal clang. The eyes of every member of the audience burned into me; fear and hatred radiated from them in waves. Guns pointed at me from all sides, no doubt loaded with silver bullets. I raised a hand. "I'm sorry, but that's the most humiliating position anyone has ever put me in." I pointed down at the hood. "Is that how you treat everyone who comes to you for help?"

"Every werewolf," the man named Rensh said. The audience around him laughed, but their laughter was uneasy and they kept their eyes and guns on me.

I shook my head. "Then maybe you aren't the right people to talk to."

I took a step toward the door, knowing it was a death sentence, but the leader held out a hand. "Wait." I turned warily. When I met his eyes he frowned but lowered his gun. "Maybe we were a bit hasty."

Mutters rose from the audience, but they quieted when he glanced at them. He steeled himself visibly. "I am Gunthrie Rogart, in charge of this assembly of Hunters. I think we need to hear what you have to say."

The sincerity in his voice, if not his words, caught my attention. He had pride, and as a leader he would do what was best for his people. As an Alpha, I could understand that. I turned to the Hunters. "My name is Jaze Carso. I am seventeen years old and a Junior in high school. I am also a werewolf, one of the last remaining Alphas that I'm aware of." Murmurs flew around the room, but I pressed on. "You are humans put into the position of Hunters to protect your loved ones." My eyes darkened. "At least two of you were involved in killing my father while working in conjunction with this werewolf who is trying to take over." I avoided looking at the two I spoke of. I didn't know if I could control myself once I saw them.

The murmurs quieted and I met Roger's eyes. He nodded and I pressed on. "If this werewolf is allowed to succeed, he will indeed have control over the entire legion of North American werewolves. We have laws in place to prevent such monopoly of the packs, but those in charge of upholding the law seem to have faded into the woodwork. Werewolves might be killable alone, but once this werewolf is fully in charge, you won't be able to get near him. We need to combine forces to stop him now before all werewolves follow him."

Angry voices rose; shouts and cries of outrage met me in a roar. I waited until Commander Rogart's gavel had brought silence once more. "He needs to be stopped, but I can't do it on my own. I need your help to wipe out this pestilence that's a danger to both our races."

Commander Rogart lifted the gavel again, but only muted talking rose around us. He studied me as he waited for the talking to die down, then nodded. "Mr. Carso," he said. Talking rose at the small token of respect he gave me, but he ignored it and pressed on. "We will discuss this matter and get back with you. We ask if you could wait in the next room and we will call you back in when we're done."

I looked around at the faces and saw a mixture of confusion, distrust, and in some places a touch of pity which surprised me. I hadn't said all that I wanted to, but I hoped maybe it was enough. I nodded. "Thank you."

Talking erupted as soon as the door shut behind me. I paced the floor and tried not to listen in. The burns around my wrists tingled, which I hoped meant they were already healing. Fresh air drifted in under the poorly fit outer door to the warehouse. I stepped toward it, toying vaguely with the idea of running before the Hunters could throw away my case and kill me instead, but a shadow crossed the thin beam of sunlight. I froze and listened. Footsteps, soft and steady. I was under guard. I felt trapped, cornered.

I forced my rising heartbeat to slow and surveyed the small room. Sawdust lay in piles in the corners, but whatever machinery had created it had been taken away long ago. A mouse squeaked in the darkness and its tail vanished inside a hole where two walls met. The roof was high with beams crossing each other well above where I could reach. I could try jumping, but worried about the sound it would make and if I could climb fast enough with my wounds.

The square panel windows were covered in cobwebs and layers of dust, and the dawn light that filtered through was weak. Particles spun and danced along the beams as if in time to music I couldn't hear. I held out a hand and watched the light splay on the floor around my shadow, lost for a moment in the simplicity of light and darkness. I thought of the battle between werewolves and Hunters and wished that in real life it could be that simple. But if so, I couldn't decide which side would be darkness and which one light.

The door opened sooner than I expected. The Hunter that opened it dropped his eyes to avoid meeting mine. Commander Rogart beckoned to me from inside the room. I stood in the door and waited a minute, knowing that if I did enter again and the atmosphere was hostile it might be the last move I made. But Commander Rogart's gun was back in its holster, and Meg and Roger's expressions were somewhat hopeful. I glanced back once at the light streaming through the windows, took a calming breath, and walked forward.

My footsteps echoed over the wooden floor, strangely loud in such a crowded but silent room. I stopped a few feet from Commander Rogart and waited quietly.

His eyes narrowed thoughtfully and a faint smile touched his lips. "You're awfully brave for a werewolf."

I smiled wryly. "I was just thinking you're pretty brave for a Hunter."

He stared at me in surprise, then laughter shook his shoulders and he chuckled until tears sparkled in his eyes. Several other Hunters in the audience joined in, and like that, tension fled the room. Commander Rogart smiled. "You're okay, kid."

"I tried to tell you I wasn't a threat when I got here," I replied.

He chuckled again and nodded. "And perhaps that would be our downfall if we didn't have reason to trust two seasoned Hunters such as Roger and Megan Valen. They vouched for your integrity and said you even saved their daughter from an attack by a pack of werewolves. Are these a part of the group you're worried about?"

I nodded. "Getting there. I'm worried Mason will have control of them soon if we don't do something."

He nodded thoughtfully and paced a few steps away, then turned and came back. He studied me as though debating whether he could trust me, then seemed to make up his mind. "Our discussions have revealed that several in this group have worked with Mason." My heartbeat quickened and I looked at the watching Hunters. Several dropped their eyes and looked away, but one or two met my gaze defiantly.

I took a deep breath and turned back to Commander Rogart. "Okay. I'll try not to hold that against them."

He smiled again so wide this time he showed pearly white teeth. "Then I think this'll work out just fine." He beckoned me closer. "I assume you have a plan?"

I nodded and began to map it out. Hunters rose from their chairs and surrounded us in order to hear better. I fought off a wave of uneasiness with so many of them near me, but Meg and Roger stood at my back, Roger's hand resting reassuringly on my shoulder. The Hunters listened carefully, several chiming in to add suggestions.

Two hours had passed by the end of the meeting. I walked out of the main room of the warehouse and felt as though something more than just a meeting with Hunters and a lone werewolf had been accomplished.

I stopped by the door and turned. "No hood and cuffs this time?" I asked the Commander who followed close behind.

He smiled again, his expression softer. "Do you know where we are?"

I nodded. "By the warehouses, the scent of a few scrappy pines and some aspen, and a bracken smell from a large body of water that must empty fairly slowly, I'd say we were near Thirty and the Loop."

His eyebrows rose appreciatively and he chuckled. "No need for the hood and cuffs then."

I pushed the door open. The morning light spilled in and turned the lonely piles of old sawdust into miniature hills of gold. I lifted my face to it and took a deep breath, then walked down to the waiting car.

Chapter 19

By the time we got home I was late for school, so I took the day off and unpacked some boxes so Mom would feel like I had accomplished something while she was gone. I put the vase with the three plastic yellow roses Dad had given Mom when he proposed to her in the middle of the table where it had been at our last house until she began to use real flowers; I hung Mom's picture of a patchwork chicken above the stove, and put the plates away in the cupboards. Mom would be glad we didn't have to use paper ones anymore.

The things I unpacked had been from our old storage unit back home, things Mom hadn't wanted to throw away when we cleaned out the garage, but had to be moved to make room for the car. These boxes were what remained of our past life, and somehow putting them up made it feel a little bit more like home.

Night slowly fell, and I felt the call of the moon although it wouldn't be full for another three weeks. I debated phasing and taking a quick run before the date, but shook off the urge with the thought that Mason was out there somewhere with his growing pack, and they would love an opportunity just like this to pick off another Alpha.

I knocked on Nikki's door an hour later. She threw it open before my hand was back down, wrapped her arms around my neck, and hugged me tight. She was shaking and I realized then how much she had truly feared for my life.

I smoothed her hair. "It's okay, Nikki; I'm okay," I reassured her.

She nodded, her face buried in my shoulder. "My parents said it went well," she replied, her voice muffled, "But it could have gone so badly."

"I know." A tremor ran up my spine at the thought of standing cuffed and hooded in the warehouse full of armed Hunters. I shook my head. "Thank goodness it's over now."

She looked up at me. "So they'll fight for you?"

I nodded. "I think we'll have a chance now."

She gave me a relieved smile, glanced over her shoulder into the living room, and grabbed something off the side table by the door. "I almost forgot," she said, her eyes shining. "I have a surprise for you."

She led the way to the detached garage and pulled it open. A red motorcycle with two helmets hanging from the handlebars stood where the car usually was. She glanced back at me. "Mom and Dad needed the car for some Hunter business. They said we could take the bike."

I stared. "You know how to drive that thing?"

She laughed. "Dad's taken me on it since I was a baby, much to Mom's horror." She tossed me a helmet and climbed on.

I shook my head and sat behind her. "So your repayment for me saving your life is to put mine in danger?"

She laughed again and kick started it. "It has been a while since I've driven," she shouted over the noise of the engine.

I grinned. "Now you tell me!"

She rolled the throttle and we shot out of the garage. I grabbed her waist to keep from being thrown off, and leaned into the turn as she rounded a corner of the road. She laughed, a carefree sound that made my breath catch, and shifted quickly to fourth. Before long, we were winding our way up a road I hadn't been on. Trees grew on either side of the two-lane road and towered over the top, blocking out the stars. The motorcycle's headlight bounced along the trunks, giving the impression that we were driving through a living tunnel.

Nikki manipulated the turns as though she had been that way many times before. She slowed when the road narrowed, then turned off onto a poorly paved road that continued through the hills. We eventually stopped before an intricately worked metal gate about a half mile in. Bars curved in the shape of wings flowed from the center and smaller wires wrapped around them like vines complete with thorns and metal leaves. Nikki shut off the engine and I took off my helmet, grateful to have my feet back on the ground and realizing at the same time that I didn't enjoy having someone else in control.

"What is this place?" I asked her.

"You'll see," she said mysteriously over her shoulder. She pushed the gates open wide enough to slip under the chain that locked them together, then turned on a flashlight and started through the trees.

I ducked in after her and stared at the magnificent trees that made up the forest behind the gate. These trees were older than the ones we had ridden through. They towered high above, ancient oaks, maples, aspen, and others I didn't know the name of but recognized by their smell. Nikki followed an overgrown path through the trees and I hurried to catch up.

She touched a trunk here and there as if they were old friends. Bushes grew thick beneath the trees so visibility beyond the path was limited to a few feet. We came upon a little clearing about five minutes up the path. A concrete statue stood in the middle surrounded by wildflowers. Nikki took a few steps toward the statue, then stopped and turned off the flashlight. The figure was illuminated by the waning moon.

"Is this a cemetery?" I asked, uncertain.

She shook her head. "A garden of saints." I walked to stand behind her and she smiled up at me. "I found it about a year ago. I come here whenever I need some peace in my life."

"So you've been here a lot," I said seriously.

She nodded and leaned back into my chest. I wrapped my arms around her and she sighed. "It's peaceful here."

I nodded. Even the breeze felt reverent the way it flowed around us warm and soft as though a sigh from heaven. I took a deep breath and let it out slowly. The peace of the quiet woods chased away some of the torment of my rushing thoughts. Nikki stepped out of my arms and took my hand. I followed her along the winding path through the trees and past several more statues, all in various states of being taken by the forest surrounding them. Moss grew up the gray carved robes of one figure, while vines twisted up another. Leaves carpeted the ground around each and flowers and shrubs rose from the forest floor as if in their own praise of the ancient saints.

The path cleared again and a saint formed of white concrete with birds on his arms and a deer at his feet stood before us. The statue itself was unimpressive; sticks had been entwined in the crook of one arm to create a nest that now stood empty. Branches fallen from a windstorm leaned on one side of the statue, and parts of its face had been worn away by the weather so that its features were mostly indistinguishable. But something about the way the cement birds and the deer had been crafted caught my attention.

"Which saint is this?" I asked quietly.

Nikki smiled and touched one of the deer's ears. "Saint Francis of Assisi, patron saint of the animals." She petted one of the carved birds lightly. "It was said that he saved a town from a wolf by making them friends instead of enemies."

I smiled and stepped into the clearing. "Oh really?"

"According to legend," she replied with a twinkle in her eyes.

She sat down in the thick grass and patted the ground near her invitingly. "Sounds like a good legend," I said, eying the statue.

She nodded. "It would be handy, wouldn't it?"

"For a saint to come tell the werewolves and humans to play nice?" She nodded again and I gave a small smile. "It definitely would."

She glanced at me out of the corner of her eye. "Do you think it'll ever happen?"

I hesitated at the hint of hope in her voice and spoke carefully, "My dad always said that anyone could get along as long as there is mutual trust."

She fell silent for a few minutes. "Then that's the problem," she then said quietly. She picked up a twig and ran it through the blades of grass.

I turned to face her, surprised at the sadness of her tone.

"There will never be trust," she said, avoiding my eyes.

I caught her chin gently and tipped her head so that she looked at me. Tears filled her eyes when they met mine and sparkled in the moonlight. "Werewolves like your uncle and Hunters like my parents make it impossible."

I let go of her chin and frowned. "My uncle can be stopped, and your parents' actions were justified. I can't blame them for reacting how they did." My stomach lurched as I thought of my dad and my own reaction. "I've done the same thing."

She sniffed and looked at me. "What?"

"I'm seeking revenge," I said bluntly. "I'm going to kill Mason for what he did to my dad, the same way that your parents went after the werewolf that killed your brother."

She bowed her head against my shoulder. "Killing never fixed anything, but you're doing it to prevent him from hurting other werewolves, too."

I nodded, but knew that if it was just in revenge for my dad's death, I would do the same thing. The guilt hung heavy in my chest. I pushed the feeling down and realized that tears soaked my shoulder. "Nikki?"

She took in a shaky breath and let it out again. It ended in a sob. "I miss Randy."

I smoothed her hair and put my arms around her, pulling her against my chest. "I know." I swallowed and forced the words out, "I miss my dad, too." Hot tears stung my eyes and I looked up at the weather-damaged saint above us to keep them from spilling over. The saint's worn face stared down at me. The cement under one eye had discolored gray, making it look like the statue cried with us. I turned my face to Nikki's head and breathed deeply of her lavender shampoo-scented hair to regain control.

"How do you live without him?" Nikki asked quietly after her sobs had stopped.

I put my cheek on top of her head and closed my eyes. "I haven't been."

Her arms tightened around me. I made myself continue. "I keep telling myself when I kill Mason the pain will go away." I took another breath. "But I know it won't."

"Then why do you do it?" she asked softly.

I opened my eyes and looked at the saint above us. "To protect those who can't defend themselves, and to keep others from going through what Mom and I have."

Nikki fell silent for a few more minutes. Crickets chirped in the grass around us and cicadas began to sing. A cloud passed over the moon, throwing us in darkness. Nikki settled closer to my side under my arm. I held her silently, taking comfort that the one person who knew my whole soul, the dark thoughts that drove my actions, and the shattered remnants of my heart, accepted me for who I was. I vowed silently to protect her from what dangers and heartaches of the world I could. The thought helped pull together a few of the shredded pieces of my soul and I breathed deeper.

***

After the constellations had shifted and a new patch of stars winked down at us from the broken canopy, Nikki stood and waiting for me by the path. I rose and said a silent thank you to the saint. I wasn't a religious person, especially after what had happened to Dad, but I felt comfort under the gaze of Saint Francis, and that was worth the world in that one moment.

We made our way back to the motorcycle. Nikki left her flashlight off and held my hand, trusting me to guide her. We stepped through the gate and she picked up her helmet.

"My turn," I said.

She glanced at me to see if I was joking. "You're serious?"

I started the engine. "It's like roller skating, right?" I called over the rumble.

"What?" she asked, her eyes wide.

I laughed, "Oh, just get on." She rolled her eyes but stepped up.

I revved the throttle and the motorcycle growled underneath us. I could see the road, but the visor of the helmet cut out my sense of smell. I pushed it back and took a deep breath of the midnight air. Nikki did the same without a word, her mouth turned in a slight smile. She then put her arms around my waist.

I let out the clutch and we started down the mountain. The headlight toyed with my wolf vision, changing from light to color to gray. I eventually turned it off, which made Nikki's hold tighten but I could see much better. We flew down the road.

Nikki eventually relaxed and leaned against my back. I smiled. The wind rushing past sang in my ears and the myriad scents of a twilight forest filled my nose. I bent lower and leaned with the turns, becoming one with the movement of the motorcycle. My heart raced as though I chased a deer with the pack. Shadows of memories ran alongside us, pack members now either working for Mason or dead. I shook my head and let the night sweep them away.

I took the back roads from the hills and avoided the highway on our way home. The city's sky scrapers loomed to the right and I detoured toward them. We slowed as we entered the city limits to the building-lined streets. Nikki squeezed my arm and I stopped in an alley between a building outlined in green lights and another with golden windows that reflected the night sky. We left the motorcycle and walked along the sidewalk.

"How do you find your way so easily?" Nikki asked.

"Scent."

She looked at me, surprised. "You mean you could smell where we were going?"

I nodded and searched for a way to explain it. "Each city has a unique smell. It comes from the products made there, the type of animals that live in the homes and on the streets, the living conditions of the people, the quality of parks, the garbage facilities, the air quality and level of pollution, the sewer systems, the gardens, and the form of vehicle most frequently driven. Within the cities, the neighborhoods have their own scents, and then the houses within them." I glanced at her. "That's how the dogs you hear about that cross the country to return to their homes make it."

"They just follow the smell?" Nikki asked, her gaze thoughtful. At my nod, she pursed her lips. "That does make sense. But it takes away the mystery."

I shrugged. "Sorry."

She laughed her light, sweet laugh and took my arm. "You're forgiven, Mr. Carso."

"Why thank you, Ms. Valen."

194

We walked between the buildings to the main road and sat down on a bench next to a tree with a trunk enclosed in wire. Cars rushed past even at the late hour. Light from the moon didn't make it to the sidewalk, but the buildings were lit like Christmas trees and would have illuminated the roads even without the curved streetlights that lined the sidewalks. We stared up at the buildings and enjoyed the silence of being separate from the hustle around us.

Nikki eventually sighed. "I'd better get home. Mom and Dad will worry."

Though I didn't want it to end, I rose and offered her my hand. We walked back to the motorcycle and I drove us home.

Chapter 20

I had slept for almost an hour when the sound of footsteps on the sidewalk in front of my house woke all my senses at once. I slipped down the stairs and crouched by the window in the front room that showed the street. I always kept the window cracked for just this reason and the scent of Chet's gang, minus Chet, brought me to full alert before the first knock sounded.

I listened at the door before opening it.

"How do we know we can trust him?" a voice growled. I recognized the deep tone as Darryl. I gritted my teeth, reminding myself that he was one of Charlie Sathing's boys and that I had promised to look out for them.

"Chet trusted him," one of the others I didn't recognize replied. "That's enough for me."

"It would be," Darryl snapped.

"Hey," Max growled before a fight could break out. "None of this is helping Chet."

I opened the door. "Helping Chet how?" I asked.

The eleven werewolves on the porch stared at me; several dropped their eyes in submission. The rest bristled and backed up as though afraid I would attack them. Given the last couple of times we had met, I couldn't blame them.

Max elbowed Darryl and his brother cleared his throat. "We, um. . ." He glanced at the others, then quickly said, "Chet's gone to settle things with Mason."

"What?" I demanded, hoping I hadn't heard him right.

Max took over for his brother, staring at a point several inches to the left of my head. "Chet told us what Mason did, how he's gaining control. He wouldn't let us come with him to stop Mason."

I stared at them in disbelief. "You mean you let him go alone?"

Several members of the pack shuffled their feet and no one would meet my eyes. I growled in frustration. "After he told you that Mason was responsible for the deaths of your loved ones, your mothers and fathers, your siblings, you let Chet go alone to face him?" I narrowed my gaze, my heart thundering. "What kind of a pack are you?"

Max looked up. "He ordered us to stay!" he said defensively.

I let out a breath of frustration. As an Alpha, I never understood the follower mentality. Now I saw it as the weakness it had been cultivated to be in the werewolf lifestyle. "Individual wolves in a wild pack still have to think for themselves," I growled. "Survival of the fittest also means of the smartest. You have to learn to think for yourselves in order to save yourselves." I leaned against the door as I sorted out my options. The pack waited, all eyes now on me. I looked at Max. "Do you know where he went?"

Max nodded and gestured to another member of the pack, Shane, the one Meg had shot. His cast was gone but he still favored his arm as though the silver pained him. I knew exactly how he felt. The blond-haired boy with freckles across his nose handed me a scrap of yellow paper. It had been carefully shaded with pencil to bring out the outline of a message that had been written on a paper on top of it. Max pointed at it with his chin. "Chet wrote down the address and took it with him. It was Shane's idea to use the impression from the page underneath."

I glanced at the address. It wasn't far. "Let me get some things and we'll go."

"All of us?" Darryl asked, his voice guarded.

I nodded. "You owe it to your Alpha to save him when he gets into sticky situations. He looks out for you, you look out for him. That's what a pack is for." I turned away and left them at the door.

It took one turn around the house for me to realize that what I really needed was at the Valens. I walked past the werewolves and crossed our lawn to go next door. Darryl and Max hurried after me, the rest of the wolves trailing behind. "You're going to the Hunters for help?" Max asked with barely concealed scorn.

I turned back to him and snapped, "They'll be more help than you were planning to be."

He stopped and fell back a few steps, then hurried to catch up to me. "It's not like we haven't done anything. We came to you, didn't we?"

I nodded. "Yes, you did. Now you need to trust me and not second-guess every move I make."

Max and Darryl both nodded and fell silent. They waited with the rest of the pack at the end of the sidewalk while I made my way up the steps to the Valen's porch.

Meg answered on my third knock. She looked out past me and her eyes widened. "We knew there were werewolves about, but we didn't know they were with you."

I quickly explained about Chet and she backed up so I could talk to Roger. I noticed she left the door open in case any of the pack wanted to come in, and was awed by her complete change of attitude toward werewolves. I was glad, though, that none of the pack tried to enter. It wouldn't be the best time to push things.

I heard footsteps in the hall as I explained the situation to Roger. "You'll probably want to hear this, too, Nikki," I said.

She stepped around the corner, her cheeks red. Her mom gave a look of disapproval, but I filled her in on what she missed. As soon as I finished, she grabbed her shoes from the closet and sat down on a chair to pull them on.

"What are you doing?" I asked in alarm.

"Coming with you, what do you think?" she shot back. "You're not tackling the biggest pack of wolves in America by yourself."

I caught her hand to keep her from tying the laces. She tried to pull away, but I wouldn't let go. "Nikki?" She finally looked at me. "I can't let you come with me," I said quietly. I glanced above her head and met Roger's gaze. He nodded in agreement.

Nikki tore her hand from my grasp and continued tying the bow with quick, jerky movements. "You aren't going without me, Jaze Carso. I won't have you killed if I can stop them."

I knelt down and grabbed both her hands in my own. "Nikki, I need you to listen to me."

When she finally met my gaze, her jaw was clenched and tears brightened her eyes. I forced myself to continue. "I can't protect myself or Chet or any of the other wolves if I'm worried about your safety." I took a deep breath. "You're my world and I can't lose you. I have a bigger risk of being killed with you there because I'll be worried about you instead of what's going on. I need to be focused in order to stop Mason. I need you to stay here, for both our sakes."

She bit her lip, her eyes searching mine as though trying to find any hint that I was lying to her. But all she saw was honesty and the pain that losing her would bring me. I wouldn't survive it if anything happened to her, not this close to losing Dad and having my whole world crash down around me.

She finally let out a ragged breath. "Come back to me," she whispered. I nodded and she leaned down, kissed me on the forehead, and left to her room. I listened for the door to slam, but it closed softly behind her. The door creaked as she leaned against it, and I heard her take a calming breath. I wanted more than anything to follow her and give her the real kiss she deserved, but knew it would be that much harder to leave her if I did. I gritted my teeth and turned back to Roger.

He grunted and picked up a phone. "I'll call in the Hunters," he said. He tipped his head toward the garage. "Grab what weapons you'll need."

I shook my head. "I haven't trained with any of them."

Meg appeared from around the corner that led to the storage room; I couldn't remember when she had left. She carried two small guns, a harness with four silver knives, and several things that looked like grenades attached to a strap. "Take these at least. I've wrapped the hilts on the knives so the silver won't bother you, you're alright with a gun, and the smoke grenades are self-explanatory."

I hesitated, then thanked her and fastened the harness around my chest so that the hilts of the knives would be accessible for a quick draw, shoved the two guns behind my belt, and strapped the grenades across my chest in the opposite direction of the knives. Roger handed me a thin black trench coat to hide the weapons. I pulled it on and a strange scent touched my nose. I glanced at him.

"It's been treated with a variety of oils to hide your scent. You don't want anyone recognizing you before you locate Chet," Roger explained, worry in his voice.

I gave them both a reassuring smile. "I'll see you guys there," I told them. "I might need a distraction, but I don't want any werewolves hurt if we can help it."

Meg and Roger watched from the door until I met up with the pack, then the couple turned quickly away. They would have their hands full rallying the Hunters days earlier than expected.

The door opened again. "Jaze?" I turned in time to see Roger toss out a set of keys. I caught them and met his eyes. "Take care of yourself," he said in a stern, fatherly tone. I blinked at the unexpected reminder of my own father and turned away before my emotions could betray me.

The garage was already open when I reached it. I started the motorcycle and gunned it past Chet's pack who already waited in their own cars parked in front of my house. The address in my head cycled over and over in time to the rhythm of the road. I turned off the freeway to find the football stadium that had been abandoned two years ago. It loomed off the freeway like a hulking giant, alone in the middle of nowhere with an empty parking lot surrounding all sides. The stadium had been scheduled for demolition, but the date kept getting pushed back until most believed it would be a relic of the city for years to come.

I drove through the huge, empty parking lot and circled the perimeter. The gates were locked and I wondered how Chet got in. Then an engine revved and Max crashed through the fence in his truck a few feet away. I shouted my thanks and he gave a wolfish grin and a military salute.

I was supposed to wait for the Hunters, but my thoughts warred between worry for Chet and my own stubbornness in not wanting to listen to others' orders. It was an Alpha thing and something Dad and I had butted heads about on more than one occasion. I parked the motorcycle near the main doors and practiced self-control by pacing the perimeter and deciding which door would be the least conspicuous to break into. Mason had somehow turned on the power to the building, and lights flooded the interior, making the stealth required for my plan a bit more difficult.

A ramp down the back   led to a huge loading door for

semi trucks. Next to it was a normal sized door whose lamp had burned out. I crouched in the shadows and watched the door for several minutes. Eventually, it opened and two men armed to the teeth stepped out. They lit cigarettes and the scent of their second-hand smoke along with the musk of werewolf drifted past my hiding place.

I debated for a few seconds. The Hunters should arrive any minute. I could either wait and let us all go in blind to whatever situation Mason had set up, or I could scope the place out and possibly make it safer for the Hunters. I pulled one of Meg's improvised smoke grenades off the strap and tossed it down the ramp, then picked up several rocks and threw them one at a time at the loading door. After the third rock hit, the werewolves ran out into the smoke, guns out and their eyes searching blindly.

I ran down the ramp with my hand on the wall closest to the door, holding my breath and with my eyes closed. I stepped swiftly and lightly, feeling my way past them and into the building. When I reached inside, I pulled the door shut and jammed a chair underneath the handle from the inside.

The werewolves banged on the door, but the smoke also contained one of Meg's mild ether formulations and a few seconds later I heard the thud of two bodies as the werewolves passed out. I checked Nikki's phone she had let me borrow so her parents could text me when the Hunters arrived, but no message had come. I tried to call Meg and Roger to warn them about the firepower the werewolves had, but the signal wouldn't go through. I gritted my teeth against a stab of worry, slipped the phone back into my pocket, and crept through the bright room, wishing for darkness. Even though the other werewolves would be able to see as good as I could, I felt better fighting in the dark; but I reminded myself that lack of light would hinder the Hunters and I was fortunate Mason had seen fit to light their way.

I left the loading room and walked down a long hallway. The walls had been stripped of cameras, for which I was grateful, and bare neon lights hummed above me. I walked carefully, every sense alert for the slightest sound. Exhaustion warred with adrenaline through my body. It had been a long few days with meeting Chet at school, talking to the Hunters, going on a date with Nikki, and now prowling around an abandoned stadium just after midnight. I needed every fiber of my body to be ready for attack, and the lack of sleep definitely came at the worst possible time.

A footstep scuffed in the next hall and I slipped into a closet just in time to avoid two sentries. Metal clicked on metal and I pictured them as armed as the two at the door had been, machine guns possibly loaded with a thousand silver bullets and tipped with silver bayonets, grenades, and the occasional serrated knife waiting to slide between a pair of ribs. Each werewolf was a walking arsenal. I wondered if Mason expected me tonight, or if he was always this cautious.

The guards passed and I slipped back out into the hallway. It was only a matter of time before they came back around or discovered the blocked doorway by the loading ramp. I could only hope the Hunters arrived soon. I checked Nikki's phone again; there was no message and I wondered if the stadium interfered with the reception.

Two hallways down I came to a set of stairs that led up. An elevator waited next to the stairs and the numbered lights at the top indicated that it was on the third level and I stood in the lowest level of the basement. I walked slowly up the stairs with a knife in one hand. I didn't like being armed, having practiced every day without weapons, but with the state of my body, I knew I couldn't take a chance.

I stepped onto the upper basement floor and voices drifted down the hallway. A strange litter of chaos filled the hall. Televisions, stereo systems, motorcycles, computers, guitars, game systems, operating equipment, speakers, all of it high end and very expensive, cluttered every available space. The air smelled of electronic wiring and gasoline, new plastic and metal, along with the scent of sweat and excitement from werewolves.

I stepped past the disorder carefully, my attention on where I placed my feet, when a familiar laugh rang out. I froze, every cell in my body springing to full attention. A growl rose in my throat and I barely remembered to keep silent. My fingers ached to tear out Mason's throat, my teeth begged to sink into his jugular and end the torment he had caused of my life. A shudder ran through my body and I crouched. I closed my eyes and concentrated on taking deep breaths, but the need to phase surged so strong I felt my teeth elongate and muzzle start to grow despite my actions.

I thought of Nikki, of our time together in the saints' meadow and on the motorcycle, of walking through the night-lit city with a hundred cars streaming by and the peace of our own silence surrounding us like a bubble. I remembered the smell of her hair and the brush of her hand against mine. With careful concentration, I was able to will my heartbeat to slow and the phase to reverse before I gave everything away. When I was sure I had my instincts under control, I stood carefully back up, thankful that no one had chosen that moment to patrol the jumbled hallway.

I sent a quick text to Nikki's parents describing my location and where Mason was, but I had little hope that the messages were getting through this far below the stadium. I made sure the phone was on vibrate and slipped it back into my pocket, then unhooked one of the smoke grenades and stepped quietly forward.

A set of double doors stood open about halfway down the hall. The scent of old sweat mingled with new, and rubber mats and a few battered helmets had been tossed out the door. Leave it to Mason to take up residence in an old football locker room. I shook my head at his lack of taste and slid against the wall by the door.

A stainless steel desk sat near the opposite wall. I crouched carefully down and tried to make sense of the distorted reflection. I eventually gave up and broke a rear-view mirror off of a nearby motorcycle and used it to see into the room. My heart fell at the sight of almost a hundred werewolves both in wolf and human form crammed into the low-ceilinged locker room.

Lifting the mirror high, I could barely make out the form of Mason sitting at the far end, several werewolves in wolf form lounging around him. More of the expensive items littered the room; a high end projector showed Scarface on one wall while werewolves cheered and played a bloody shooter on another. I couldn't see Chet anywhere. I had counted on Mason to keep him nearby. A shard of worry laced through me that perhaps Mason had already killed him, but my instincts told me Mason planned on me coming after Chet. He would wait to finish the Alpha until I was near.

I had to alter my plan a bit. It was one thing to step out and declare Alpha Accord and hope that every werewolf in the stadium knew the law and would uphold it; it was far another to realize that the reason Mason hadn't been punished for breaking the laws was probably because the elders who upheld them were either killed or out of commission in some way or other. The thought made me feel extremely alone.

I could throw a grenade and hope to knock them all out, but by the smell I could tell that there were at least double the number of werewolves wandering around the stadium either on patrol or fooling around with the numerous entertainment items that lay piled up everywhere. I could hope that declaring myself an Alpha and challenging Mason would be enough for the other werewolves to back down and let us have it out, or I could just go in guns blazing and hope to take down as many as I could in the hopes that the Hunters would clean up the rest.

All the options twisted my stomach. There had to be another way. I just couldn't-

An explosion sounded and the entire stadium shook. Cries of terror rose from the werewolves, twisting to hysteria when a second explosion rang out. I leaned against the wall for support and tried to keep my balance when a third blast sounded. Something whined high in the air, then the sounds faded to leave only cries of terror and pain around the stadium. My pocket vibrated and I pulled out the phone.

'Hunters have arrived', Meg's text said and I could imagine her dry tone. I rolled my eyes and fought back a smile as I shoved the phone back in my pocket. I crouched back down just before werewolves started to swarm from the locker room.

I searched the crowd for Mason, worried that he would slip out another way or stay in the room with bodyguards, but then a form in a tailored black suit ran past. I bit back a snarl and fell in behind him, pretending to be as panicked as the rest of the werewolves until we pooled at the bottom of the stairs while everyone scrambled to escape.

I put a knife to Mason's back and he froze. "Let out a sound and I'll plunge this so far through your spine you'll never heal," I growled in his ear. I grabbed his arm and pulled him back with me through the hysterical crowd. No one noticed us in their haste to escape, and only just before we reached another door did werewolves start to look around for Mason.

The door behind me was locked, but I broke the handle and pulled Mason with me into a short, branching hallway that turned to the right and left a few feet away. I pulled the door shut behind us and Mason used the distraction to slip out of my grip and elbow me in the chin. Stars danced before my eyes. I turned with my hands up and the knife out ready for another attack, but he knew better than to face a full Alpha head on.

Chapter 21

Mason ran down the short hall and the stars cleared just enough for me to see him turn left at the end. I slipped the knife into its sheath and ran after him. I turned left, then dove back down the hall when a hail of bullets peppered the walls around me.

"Think I'm dumb enough to go unarmed when there's an Alpha after my hide?" Mason shouted, his tone taunting.

My lips lifted in a silent snarl at the sound of his voice, but I didn't reply. I pulled a grenade from my chest and was ready to throw it when the sound of footsteps echoed down the hall. The coward was running again.

I took off after him, my heart pounding and adrenaline coursing so strong I almost gave in to the phase only to meet another spray of bullets around the next corner. I slid against the wall and cursed the fact that I didn't know the layout of the stadium well enough to circle around and intercept him. I could easily lose him or he could catch up to his bodyguards before we met up again.

"Fight like an Alpha if you're going to be an Alpha," I yelled, letting my frustration show in my voice.

"If I get rid of you and Chet there aren't many others who could stand in my way," Mason called back, followed by another volley of bullets. His footsteps sounded again before the echo of the bullets ceased. I took off running and rounded the next corner in time to see him disappear into a door on the left.

I pulled out one of my guns and barreled into the door with my shoulder. Bullets sprayed around me and one tugged at the sleeve of my trench coat before I ducked behind a wide ledge that smelled like it was used to serve refreshments to the players. I fired above the ledge without looking and listened to the bullets hit various metal pieces and softer objects.

"Got a gun like the big boys, huh Jaze?" Mason called out, his voice edged with anger.

"Guns are for cowards," I yelled back. "I'm stooping to your level to prove you're not the only one that can fight like a weasel."

A snarl ripped from his lips and a faint gleam of triumph rose in my chest. He and Dad used to argue with pulled punches and half barbs, but weasel was the one thing Mason never took well to being called. It was a werewolf term to mock those not of full blood, and my Dad's way of reminding Mason of his place. I wondered for the first time if they were not full brothers.

"You don't know who you're messing with," Mason growled, the ferocity in his voice so thick the hair rose on the back of my neck.

"I could say the same about you," I said quietly.

Another rumble shook the stadium and a light fell from the ceiling, hitting the floor in a shower of sparks. I threw a grenade during the distraction, but Mason was a step ahead of me. Smoke filled the room just as he ducked out a side door I hadn't noticed. I pulled my shirt up to cover my nose, closed my eyes, and ran with my hand on the wall to the door. I ducked through just as the ether began to flow.

I shoved the door shut behind me and leaned against the opposite wall to give my head a chance to clear. My arm ached and my sleeve was damp; a quick check showed that the bullet had cut a deep groove just below my shoulder but went straight through without leaving many silver shards. Blood trickled down my arm and dripped off my fingers, but I didn't have time to deal with it. Spots flashed before my eyes from the sparks and I couldn't shake the dizziness from the smoke and the blow Mason had landed to my chin, but every second I waited he grew further away.

I pushed off the wall, stumbled against it, then regained my footing. I held my gun low in my right hand, unsheathed a knife and carried it in my left. I was done fooling around. Mason was too dangerous, and any thought of mercy fled at the touch of more blood from his hands.

I ran up the hallway and followed his scent to the elevator. The light stopped at level three and I wondered who would be stupid enough to ride an elevator in a stadium currently being bombed, but his scent disappeared inside and the elevator didn't come back down. I took a steeling breath and ran up the stairs. Adrenaline drove me and a feral smile touched my lips at the thought of finally bringing Mason to an end.

The third level turned out to be the highest in the stadium; werewolves pushed past me to get down the stairs and outside. No one seemed to notice my gun and knives, but so many of the werewolves were armed I actually fit. I shoved between a cluster of wolves at the head of the stairs and reached the top in time to see Mason push another button in the elevator.

Another explosion sounded and the force threw me against the railing. Several werewolves screamed and everyone ran in a mad rush down the stairs. I climbed onto the railing, jumped across the crowd to the other side, then half-ran, half-slid my way down the hand rail to the second floor.

The door was only halfway open and the elevator had stopped just below the edge. I could see Mason stalking agitatedly across the floor.

"Give up, Mason," I yelled up to him. "Maybe I'll show you the mercy you never gave my father."

"I didn't want to kill my own brother," he answered. The sound of metal on metal followed. "But he gave me no choice."

"There's always a choice," I shouted. My vision flared red and my heart thundered in my chest. I shoved the gun into the opening at the bottom of his elevator and pulled the trigger so many times the clicking of empty chambers didn't register until the red haze faded.

I put a foot on each side of the door and used it to lift me up so I could see inside. The acrid smell of gunpowder filled the elevator, but that was all. Mason had pulled himself through the roof.

I cursed my stupidity and ran back up the stairs. I shoved the barrel of my empty gun between the doors and pried them apart. The elevator shaft below me looked empty until movement behind the elevator caught my eye. I jumped and landed half a story down onto the elevator with a jarring thud that made every pain in my body explode to life. I lowered myself down the side in time to see Mason disappear back out the partly opened door to the second floor.

I threw myself toward the door, caught the edge with an answering stab of pain through my ribs, and pulled myself up. Mason waited with a half-smile, his dark brown eyes, the same color as my dad's, were cold and contained an animosity and hatred that never would have filled my father's.

"Attack," Mason growled.

My heart slowed as close to twenty werewolves around him surged toward me. I grabbed the only chance I had and yelled, "Alpha Accord."

The werewolves slowed and threw confused glances back at Mason. He stared at me, his eyes narrow.

"Alpha Accord," I repeated. "You want to be the Alpha, you follow the Alpha laws."

"What if I killed the elders who made the laws?" he replied with a triumphant, toothy grin.

I swallowed to push down the fear that streaked through my bones. "So you call yourself an Alpha, but throw aside any law that governs werewolf conduct? Then what makes them follow you?"

His lips pulled back in a snarl. "I'm the strongest, so they have to follow me."

The werewolves looked from him to me, following our conversation closely. I pushed away any pain, fear, and any reluctance I had and stood straight and proud. "I am the only true Alpha in this building if you've already killed Chet. They won't follow you unless you kill me." He raised his gun, but I took a chance and grabbed the strap that released the knife harness and grenades from my chest and let them fall to the ground, then I tossed both my guns on top of it. "Alphas fight to the death with nothing but their wits and brawn," I reminded him.

He stared at me and a faint spark of reluctant respect showed in his eyes when he finally nodded. The werewolves surrounding us both gave him no choice, and we both knew that, but he made a show of setting down his gun and tossing a myriad of knives and other weapons I hadn't known he carried onto the pile. "Fine, a fight to the death, then. May the strongest werewolf win," he declared. There was a strange catch to his tone as if he was still trying to pull something over on me, but when he moved in, his expression was deadly serious.

He lunged in an effort to knock me down, but I jumped out of the way, then spun back with a kick that caught him across the jaw. He didn't fall, but staggered backward with a surprised expression. "You fight dirty like your father," he said, his gaze dark.

A growl burst from my chest and I barreled him into the wall with my shoulder and slugged him twice in the stomach before he pushed me back. "Don't you dare talk about my father," I said in a voice so low and angry I barely recognized it.

I ducked a left. He swung a right roundhouse that caught me in the ribs right where the knife had gone in during my fight with Chet's pack. The air left me in a rush and I fell to the ground clutching my side. Mason caught me behind the ear with another right, then kicked at me, but I managed to get my wits about me and blocked his kick with my forearms. I grabbed his foot with both hands, ducked under it, and rose while sweeping out with my own foot to catch him just below the knee. He spun horizontally and landed heavily on the ground.

I jumped on him and wrapped an arm around his throat, pulling back hard with my other hand so that he bowed backward with my knees against his spine. He sputtered something that sounded like, "Wait!"

I didn't want to let go. Every inch of my being screamed for me to pull back further and break his spine, ending the destruction he had spread through every inch of my world. But it didn't feel right. Instinct told me that something was off and I needed to listen.

I slowly eased him down to the point where he could talk. "Speak," I growled into his ear.

"Chet," he gasped out.

"What about him?" I demanded.

He motioned and I pulled him to his feet. The motion pulled angrily at my stomach, but I ignored it. He motioned again and I walked with him to the wide stretch of windows that overlooked the brown grass of the retired stadium grounds. Shadows of players, memories of points scored and games won, hearts broken and heroes made, haunted the darkness where the faded stadium lights no longer reached, but in the clearing on the brown grass that had once been proud turf beneath cleats and leather, lay the still form of Chet surrounded by at least fifty werewolves who stayed firm to Mason's orders despite the stadium exploding around them.

"My werewolves will kill him if you kill me," he said with a hint of triumph in his voice.

"What makes you think I care if you kill him?" I asked in a growl.

"You're here, aren't you?" he pointed out. Then he slipped something out of his sleeve and turned faster than I thought he could. I raised my left arm in time to feel the slice of silver run from my wrist to my elbow, leaving my trench coat sleeve in tatters.

"Playing fair?" I asked angrily. I shrugged out of the coat and let it fall to the floor. Blood streamed down my arm.

A dark shadow crossed the window behind Mason, blocking out the bright stadium light for the briefest second. I tipped my head so I could see around him, and my heart soared at the sight of Hunters streaming down both sides of the field.

"Who said we need to play fair?" Mason growled, missing the shadow. He tore off his shirt and jumped at me.

But I was ready. My body bent, my teeth grew, and in a split second I was in wolf form, my black hair standing on end and a growl of such menace rolling from my chest that the werewolves around us backed up to the far ends of the hallway.

I met Mason tooth to tooth as he tried to tear out my eyes and blind me or reach my jugular. But I was an Alpha, and I was stronger. I forced him back and his eyes widened. I shoved him so that he staggered backwards, then lunged low and clamped onto one of his hind legs.

He tore at my shoulder, but I didn't feel the pain past the red haze that fueled my thoughts. I bit down until the bones snapped and he let out a howl, then I shook my head and he smashed into a wall and climbed slowly back to his three good feet. He growled, low and angry, realizing I was about to take everything away from him that he had tried so hard to create. His eyes rolled and any normalcy he had shown disappeared behind a crazed glaze. Foam flecked his dark gray muzzle when he snarled.

I faked a lunge forward; when he jumped to meet my attack, I leaped to the side, using my shoulder to shove him over onto his back. Before he could right himself, I clamped onto his throat and bit down. Blood pooled around my muzzle. Mason whined in protest, his tail between his legs and his feet kicking for any purchase. His breath wheezed in his throat and his blood pounded millimeters from my fangs.

Chapter 22

A step sounded to my right and I glanced over to see that the twenty or so werewolves who had been ready to tear me apart were now in wolf form, watching the fight and waiting for the moment when I would release Mason and give the defeated would-be Alpha to them so they could rip him to shreds. It was werewolf law that any Alpha who challenged another Alpha and lost was destroyed by those he wanted to lead.

But I had lost all respect for the law. I released Mason's neck slowly and growled a warning for him to remain still. He froze, his neck out and paws in the air, a humiliating position for any werewolf, but one that could save his life if he did as I instructed. The werewolves around me stepped forward, gray heads lowered and teeth eager to rip into flesh. I snarled, fierce and angry at the laws, the situation, and the faint shard of humanity that whispered that I wasn't a killer, that I wouldn't stoop to Mason's level.

The wolves backed off immediately, confusion in their eyes but their heads bowed respectfully. I phased back to my human form, then stood slowly and pulled on the tattered remains of my shirt and pants. The blood from my arm dripped to the floor. I hesitated, then pulled on the trench coat, too. It wouldn't do to appear injured to the wolves.

I glared at the animals around me and they dropped their eyes submissively. "No one is to kill Mason. He's mine," I said in a tone that left no room for argument. Mason stared up at me, his dark brown eyes, so like my father's, were shrewd, calculating, and filled with fear. "Phase," I growled at him. "And pull on your clothes. We have some people to meet."

He phased and put his clothes back on. I watched his reflection in the window as he bent down and attempted to slip a silver knife into his sleeve, but four big gray wolves stepped forward growling and showing their teeth. He dropped the knife and backed up quickly until he reached my side.

"Now what?" he asked; the command was gone from his tone and the whiny note that replaced it made me want to bare my teeth and snap at him.

"We're going down to the field. You first."

He stared at the swarm of Hunters that filled the brown-grassed stadium. "You've got to be kidding," he protested.

I pushed him forward through the door. "You were the first to make friends with the Hunters, remember? I just took it to the next level."

He stumbled down the two flights of stairs and I had to practically drag him down the ramp to the field. The werewolves still in wolf form from the third level followed us down, and when we stepped out on the grass, all eyes turned to us. I ignored the shiver that ran down my spine from the pain, the remnants of silver from the bullet that had grazed my arm, and the searching looks of the werewolves who hadn't seen what had happened between Mason and me.

Mason squirmed in my hold and I worried for a brief second that he would break free and call to the werewolves who were still loyal to him. I grabbed his right arm and pulled it tight behind his back, encircling his throat with my left arm as I did so. He let out a strangled protest, but walked submissively to where Chet was being attended to by Meg, Roger, and Nikki.

"Is he alright?" I asked when we drew near.

Nikki looked up at my voice and the relief that swept across her face soothed the last vestige of the urge to kill that tightened my heart the longer I was in contact with Mason.

I shoved Mason to the ground, then turned to the werewolves. Hunters stood around the perimeter of the field with guns pointed in every direction. They looked as uneasy as the werewolves, and I wondered if they all felt as amazed at the sheer numbers of each group as I did. My heart fell at the sight of so many gray wolves, but no Alphas. I glanced back at Chet. He moaned and a werewolf with short blond hair tended to him. My stomach tightened and I realized that with Chet out for a while, I was the last Alpha.

I looked down at the blood dripping from my fingers, then turned and glared at Mason. My expression must have said what I felt because his eyes dropped and he cowered against the ground, his face pale. "One Alpha shouldn't be in charge of all werewolves," I said loud enough to carry across the stadium. I turned and looked at the werewolves around us. "Just like our wolf ancestors, we were meant to run in family packs, protecting and caring for our loved ones. Return to your homes." Several heads lifted as though they would protest, but I continued, "I'll be holding quarterly meetings with your chosen Alphas until the young black coats grow old enough to take their rightful positions."

"How do we know who's fit to lead?" someone shouted.

I gave Mason a smile cold as ice. "The smartest, fastest, and bravest should always lead. That's the way it is in the wild, and the way it will be here. If someone is fit to lead, they will be prepared to fight for it." I met as many eyes as I could. "But thanks to Mason's work we are dangerously low in number. Don't kill each other. Accept leadership as long as you are being led in the right direction." I paused and my eyes narrowed, "And if you're being led wrongly, have the courage to stand up." Several werewolves nodded and dropped their eyes in embarrassment; I noted Chet's pack among them and fought back a smile.

"Go back to your homes and live in peace with the humans. The war with the Hunters ends now on both sides. If you try to keep it up, I will find out and I will put an end to any trouble." Murmurs arose and I held up a hand. "I've come to an agreement with the Hunters. They hunt us because we are a threat to their families." Arguing broke out, but the werewolves fell silent when I continued, "Just as they are a threat to ours. We can continue as we are, fighting and killing each other until the next generation comes back to retaliate, or we can work together to keep our loved ones safe."

I searched through the audience until I found Commander Rogart among the armed Hunters near the entrance to the field. He gave one short nod. I swept my eyes over the field of werewolves and Hunters and raised my voice so that everyone would have no doubt as to my words. "As far as I know, I am the last Alpha, and in this my word is law. We will work with the Hunters and not against them. We will keep our packs safe and the presence of werewolves as hidden from the world as much as we can. We will work to protect each other and keep our race safe from harm."

My gaze turned threatening. "We will not harm humans, and any werewolf found guilty of such will be punished accordingly." I let the threat hang in the air for a moment, then smiled to lighten the mood. "Today begins a new era for werewolves and Hunters alike. It'll take time to work out the trust issues for both species, but in the end we will all be safer for it. Get to know your neighbor, learn to coexist, and we will all be alright."

My words hung in the air and I could feel the tension of both the werewolves and Hunters at my challenge. It was tenuous and I knew I walked a fine line.

A clear, deep voice rumbled out. "The Hunters accept Jaze Carso's offer of peace," Commander Rogart said.

Hunters and werewolves alike voiced their opinion of his words, but he raised a hand and they quieted. "If acceptable per Mr. Carso, we will hold a monthly meeting with the werewolf Alphas to work out our issues and see where we can help in controlling any situations in need of both of our skills."

I heard a few werewolves grumble that they had all the skills we would ever need, but I silenced them with a look and nodded at the Commander. "That would work out well. We'll convene at the end of each month in the old warehouse on Thirty and the Loop, and any problems will be discussed then." Commander Rogart smiled at the irony and nodded.

Exhaustion swept through me and the blood had started to thicken down my arm. I fought back the urge to rub my eyes and took a steeling breath. "Go back to your homes, choose your Alphas, and we'll reconvene in two weeks. It won't be easy, but peace between the Hunters and werewolves will bring far greater security than you have yet experienced. My father was killed by Hunters who conspired with Mason, and so this ends now in his name. Peace with the Hunters begins today, and anyone who doesn't comply will answer to me."

I turned away to indicate that I was through talking as much because I was too tired to come up with anything else that needed to be said as because I was concerned about Chet and wanted to make sure he was alright. But I turned and looked straight into the eyes of my uncle and knew that my problems weren't over.

Mason stood on his feet, a burning hatred in his eyes and his fists clenched. Mouse stood between us and Meg and Roger had guns pointed at him, but he didn't seem to notice.

"Don't be stupid," I told him quietly, my eyes never leaving his. "If you attack me now, I'll have to kill you. You've left me no choice."

A strange smile appeared on Mason's face and his eyes rolled slightly. "You said there was always a choice." He charged at me, hands out and lips pulled back in a snarl.

I made a split second decision, ducked under his charge, then stood, throwing him into the pack of werewolves who had followed me from the third level. Mason's body disappeared beneath teeth and claws. I turned away, sick to my stomach. I had made a different choice, but it wasn't one I wanted.

Nikki put a hand on my arm. "You did what you had to."

Her touch soothed the ache in my heart. I tipped Nikki's face to mine, and kissed her soundly. She froze in surprise, then kissed me back with an intensity that stole my breath. I pulled her into a hug and she rested her head against my chest. I looked up to see Meg and Roger standing over Chet. Roger just shrugged and the hint of a resigned smile showed on Meg's face.

Chet groaned and I let go of Nikki and lowered to my knees beside him. "Is he going to be okay?" I asked the female werewolf with short blond hair who had been tending to him. She checked his pulse and the rate of blood flow from wounds in his shoulder and side. "He should be okay if we get the bullets out," she said. "I work at the hospital and have some friends that are, uh, friendly to werewolves." She watched me, worried that she had crossed a line. But she definitely wasn't the first to break the law against humans knowing of our presence, and I wouldn't be the one to reinforce it.

I nodded. "Thank you; let's get him there. I appreciate your help."

She wadded up a handkerchief and held it against his wounds. I turned to the other werewolves and singled out three at the front. "Give her whatever assistance is needed to get him to the hospital."

The werewolves stepped forward immediately. They lifted Chet carefully from the ground and carried him off. I watched them leave the field, my head spinning. Werewolves began to talk among themselves and the Hunters apparently decided it was safe to leave the stands. Commander Rogart walked warily across the field, several Hunters, Charlie Sathing included, at his side.

Brock ran over from the stands, his eyes wide and face pale in obvious concern at being caught in the middle of so many werewolves. "That was awesome!" he said when he reached me. He leaned over breathlessly and put his hands on his knees. "I need to stop eating so much pizza." He took several deep breaths, then stood back up. "I've decided to become a Hunter."

Nikki and I stared at him. "What made you decide that?" I asked, surprised.

He gestured around the stadium. "Have you seen their guns? Where else will I get to blow things up and carry awesome weapons?"

I laughed and searched the crowd near us. "Hey, Meg?" When she turned, I grinned. "I think I've found you a new recruit." At her questioning look, I tipped my head to indicate Brock.

Her brow lowered and she turned away without commenting.

"What?" Brock asked.

Nikki and I laughed again. "Don't be offended," I reassured him. "She's had a rough day. I hear she's a good trainer."

"Really?" he asked, excited.

Nikki shook her head. "Not really. She'll run you ragged."

He backed up quickly and made an excuse about needing to talk to Mouse before disappearing into the crowd.

"You up for a quiet drive?" Nikki asked with a gentle smile.

I nodded, longing for the silence of the woods. "Can I borrow your motorcycle?" I asked Roger.

He smiled. "Definitely."

Meg touched my arm, her expression stern. "But not before we take care of this."

I reluctantly shrugged out of my trench coat and handed it to Roger, who smiled wryly at the tears and folded it over his arm. Nikki's gaze tightened with concern at the gash down my arm and the bullet graze, but both wounds had already begun to heal.

Meg brought out a bag of tools and I avoided looking at them too closely. Nikki grabbed my hand and my fingers closed impulsively at the digging of a cold instrument as Meg removed the shards of silver. She then wrapped both wounds in bandages. "What about that?"

She pointed to the back of my shoulder. When I touched it with my hand, my fingers came away damp and I remembered the bite of Mason's teeth when we had fought in wolf form. I shook my head. "They're just bite marks, no silver to worry about." Meg gave me a stern gaze that would make an Alpha proud and I finally turned around so she could tend to it. She made me pull off my shirt and I gritted my teeth when the cloth caught against the wound.

I watched the werewolves leave the grounds slowly while Meg patched me up. A few nodded at the waiting Hunters, which I took to be positive, but most just ignored them and left as quickly as possible. Change would take time; I just hoped they could keep the peace until we got all the details worked out.

Meg whispered quietly under her breath about stubborn werewolves, cleaned the torn skin, and bandaged it loosely. "Looks like you'll live," she said in a tone of approval. She stepped back to admire her work. "You could probably take that off in an hour or so."

I flexed my muscles and rolled the shoulder. It felt a little stiff, but the pain had already lessened to a dull annoyance. "Thank you. You're going to miss patching me up," I said teasingly.

She nodded. "Now I'll have to get a real job."

I gave her a quick hug of thanks and she paused in surprise, and then hugged me back with a tightness that showed how worried she had been.

I glanced over to find Commander Rogart watching us. I held out my hand. "Thank you, sir. I greatly appreciate your help."

He shook my hand and glanced meaningfully at the werewolves milling around the stadium. "It looks like you had things under control," he said.

I smiled because we both knew how close I had come to losing them, and how precarious our new situation was. "We have a few things to work out."

He nodded. "The meeting will be soon enough. It'll give everyone a chance to get used to things, and you deserve a break."

He nodded respectfully at Nikki. "My dear." He turned and walked away to a group of werewolves who were talking near the goal post. The werewolves watched him guardedly, but didn't show any signs of aggression. It was a start.

"Nice job," a familiar voice said behind me. I turned to find Charlie Sathing standing with his gun holstered next to his nightstick.

I smiled. "I'm glad you made it."

He kicked the dead grass on the field with the toe of his scuffed shoe. "You've done a good job here."

"We still have a lot of work to do."

"But it's a good start. Well done." He shook my hand, then turned away, but a group of werewolves by the entrance to the field caught my attention. "Mr. Sathing, wait."

He turned back and I waved my hand. Chet's pack cut through the crowd and made their way to my side. I motioned for Max and Darryl to step forward. "Mr. Sathing, I would like you to meet your sons. Max, Darryl, this is your father."

Their eyes widened and they stared each other up and down. Tears glimmered at the corners of Charlie eyes, but he didn't move as though afraid he would mess it up. An awkward silence passed between them, then Darryl grabbed Charlie up in a bear hug. I grinned and turned away to give them some privacy.

Nikki took my hand and we walked through the wolves to the ramp. We wandered slowly through the stadium that now looked like a war zone; huge chunks of cement lined the walkway, the walls were cracked, and dust from the explosions still filled the air. The multitude of expensive things Mason's werewolves had gathered now lay under debris and sparking electrical wiring. A few werewolves picked among the rubble, but most ignored it entirely and left the stadium to its own rest. Nikki slipped her arm through mine and I led her down the steps to the waiting motorcycle. I stopped the bike just outside the fence Max had been so thoughtful to bash down for me.

Cool night air blew around us, tangling Nikki's black hair and whipping mine in my eyes. I closed them and took a deep breath. The scent of trees, thick grass, and the promise of rain chased away the last few shreds of dread in my stomach.

"You okay?" Nikki asked.

I nodded. "I am." I opened my eyes and realized it was the first time that was true since Dad died. I steered the motorcycle across the dark parking lot. The howls of wolves followed us and a smile touched my lips.

Chapter 23

We parked the bike on the path, then walked through the trees that swayed gently in their evening dance. We settled at the base of the St. Francis statue secure in the night and the peace of being completely alone. Nikki cuddled under my arm.

"You sure I'm not hurting you?" she asked.

I leaned my chin on the top of her head. "Not one bit."

She traced patterns on the back of my hand and answering shivers ran up my arm. I closed my eyes. A distant howl pierced the air. Another joined it, heading our way. The urge to phase and run with them rushed through my veins. I straightened slightly to listen. The howls sounded again, louder this time as though they came from where we had parked the motorcycle. I picked Mouse's howl out of the pack. The tone changed, calling to me. My muscles twitched in response.

"Go with them," Nikki said.

I looked over in surprise and found her watching me with knowing eyes. "It's okay," she said with a small laugh.

"I don't want to leave you alone," I protested.

She pushed my good shoulder gently. "A run would do you good."

I hesitated, glancing from her to where the wolves had fallen silent, waiting for me to decide. Nikki pushed my shoulder again. "Just come back to me."

I stood up with a laugh. "You think I could forget you?"

She looked up at me, her blue eyes sparkling with the light of the stars. My heart thumped louder and I leaned down and kissed her. She kissed me for a few seconds, then pushed me back with a laugh. "They're not going to wait forever!"

I stepped behind a bush and phased. I hesitated before stepping back out. Even though Nikki had seen me in wolf form, it felt strange this time, like I was bearing my soul to her.

"Jaze?"

With Nikki, there was nothing left to hide.

I took a deep breath and padded silently across the moonlit grass. Nikki knelt, took my head in her hands, and bent so that her forehead rested against mine. Her fingers tangled in my thick black coat. She closed her eyes and sighed softly. "I love every part of you," she whispered quietly. She kissed my nose and stood up.

Tears stung my eyes.

"Go," she said, her smile as soft as the moonlight on my fur.

Howls started again, more wolves than I had ever heard together. The sound was haunting and beautiful, calling to the part of me that longed for midnight runs and forest chases. I looked back at Nikki. She laughed and made a shooing motion with her hands. I gave her a wolfish grin and loped into the night. There was a beautiful, sweet, gentle girl behind me, and the thrill of a moonlit night run with a loyal pack before me. I was truly alright.

About the Author

Cheree Alsop is the mother of a beautiful, talented daughter and two amazing twin sons who fill every day with light and laughter. She married her best friend, Michael, who changes lives each day in his Chiropractic clinic. Cheree is currently working as a free-lance writer and mother. She enjoys reading, riding her Ninja motorcycle on warm nights, and rocking her twins while planning her next book. She is also an aspiring drummer and bass player for her husband's garage band.

Cheree and Michael live in Utah where they rock out, enjoy the outdoors, plan great adventures, and never stop dreaming.

39574034R00129

Made in the USA
Middletown, DE
19 January 2017